RUN WITH THE HORSES

Compliments of
Tom Lindberg

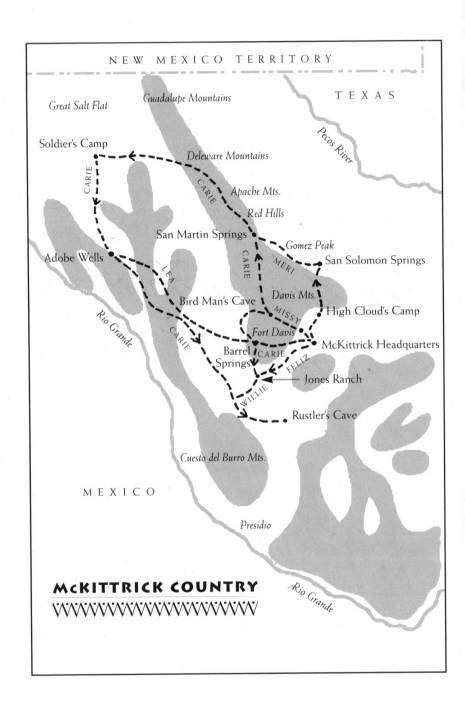

RUN WITH THE HORSES

JOAN STOCKS NOBLES

Foreword by Joyce Gibson Roach

TCU Press
Fort Worth

Library of Congress Cataloging-in-Publication Data

Nobles, Joan Stocks.
    Run with the horses / Joan Stocks Nobles ; foreword by Joyce
Gibson Roach.
        p.   cm.
    ISBN 0-87565-181-X (alk. paper)
    I. Title.
PS3564.0275R8 1998
813'.54 — dc21
                                                        97-27208
                                                             CIP

Text and Cover Design by Barbara Whitehead, Austin, Texas.
Cover photo by Wayne Baize, Fort Davis, Texas.
The photo on page 178 was taken by Ann Thoreson.

For Joe Stocks

CONTENTS

PREFACE

VVVVVVV

THIS BOOK IS RESPECTFULLY dedicated to my grandfather, Joe Stocks. He first told me the story as a child when I lay ill with red measles. We were in the huge wooden shack that was our first home on the ranch in the Davis Mountains in far West Texas. Because I was kept in quarantine and away from my only play mate, my beloved brother Banky, Daddy Stocks sat by my bed for countless days and nights, with my mother anxiously standing in the dim light at the foot of the bed. He bathed my face and small body with a wet cloth, telling me of Gran Carie and her horses. The magical tale, in his words, was a yarn, but it seemed to me, a little girl, as real as the response of my burning body to his ministering hands, and my childish mind became excited in anticipation of what happened next. In retrospect, I firmly believe it was his way to keep me alive through that awful fever, for in all my sixty-some years I can never remember being so hot

Joe Stocks was a red-headed Irishman who stood 6'2" and was hard, tough, and sometimes unkind to the extreme. To him it seemed that the chores Banky and I did were never done right; he would say, "This is what you could have done better!" Other times, he was great fun, giving us freedom to do almost anything that made

RUN WITH THE HORSES

us happy, and spending hours telling us stories, even bragging to his friends, "I can take those two kids and do anything on this ranch that needs to be done." Never, that I can remember, did he praise us directly. He had run away from home at sixteen to join the trail drives to Kansas and had lived to see the jet age. These profound extremes caused him to feel rage on the one hand and boisterous laughter on the other, as he pondered the changes wrought in his lifetime. But without a doubt, he was one of the finest ranchmen I have ever known. His registered Rambouilet sheep were sold all over the world. Mohair from his Angoras brought the best prices when sent to market, and his cattle were the envy of all. But his all-consuming passion was his Thoroughbred horses.

For many years he had used government remount stallions to raise horses and mules for the U.S. Cavalry, and he continued to do so until the cavalry disbanded in 1944. He mounted us on those tall Thoroughbreds even before our toes could reach the stirrups. We felt the fear and, yes, the pain of their great power, and we were awed by their stamina and strong hearts. Daddy Stocks believed that there was nothing that could not be accomplished through desire and the pride of hard work, and he relentlessly taught and gave all he knew to his two grandchildren. But his love of the beautiful, fleet Thoroughbred horse was branded into the heart and mind of his granddaughter. In her eyes, everything that happened to Gran Carie in the story could have and therefore did happen.

Again I had awakened curled in a hard knot, fever and chills wracking my body. Tears of frustration and self-pity began to roll down my cheeks, and I angrily reached up to brush them away. I managed to open my one good eye to glance at the clock. Four-fifteen, its merry bright light told me. Wearily, I rolled over, pushed back the warm quilts and made my way to the bathroom. With trembling hands I reached for the ever-present row of pill bottles next to the sink. The cold water from the tap eased my dry mouth, and its sweet taste began to erase the foul odor of illness. I placed the tumbler next to the medicine bottles and cupped my hands, filling them with water and, with my head bursting in pain, vigorously scrubbed my face.

My thoughts again wandered to Daddy Stocks, as they had each time I had become sick during the past six long months. When I was a child he would say, "Sweetie, you're not sick. All you need is your face washed and a good cup of coffee!" Laughing at my screaming protests he would drag me to the sink and proceed, with his work-worn hands, to scrub me with cold spring water until my skin felt raw. Throwing a towel over my now dripping head and face, he'd lead me to the kitchen table, at the same time reaching for the pan of boiled coffee that bubbled on the wood stove. I would almost gag as he poured the syrupy coffee into his large mug. But with lightning speed, my hand would dart out from under the towel to the ever-present pitcher of milk brought each morning from the "cooler." Our morning ritual was a game of who could pour milk or coffee faster. Slugging down the hated brew in huge gulps, not wanting to add more insult to my churning stomach, I'd jump up and reach for my hat that hung next to the door. As I slammed the hat down on my head, his parting words never varied: "Don't miss a one, sweetie, or I'll send you back!" Stumbling down the steps in the pre-dawn darkness, I would run up the hill to the picket corral where two "night horses" stood patiently waiting. Unbuckling a leather strap that hung on the gate post, I would open the gate, catch the nearest horse, buckle the strap around his neck and lead him to the open gate, and, using the gate as a ladder, I would climb onto the horse's back. Lightly touching my spurs to his side, I'd urge the horse off into the inky darkness. I felt perfectly safe, and I knew I wouldn't fall off, because I could feel when my mount went up or down in the rough, rolling hill "trap" of some 2,560 acres. I was also perfectly confident of my horse's keen senses of sight and hearing. Together, the horse and I would bring thirty or forty saddle horses home.

It was four o'clock in the morning.

I was nine years old.

"Well, old lady, you're not nine years old now." I straightened, deliberately not looking at my face in the mirror above the sink. I turned and made my way through the dark house, hesitating only long enough to pick up one of the quilts on my way to the kitchen to brew a pot of weak coffee in the automatic coffee-maker. Standing with the quilt clutched around me, I looked out my kitchen window. This window had been cut through a thirty-two-inch adobe wall of a house built near the turn of the century. I thought, as I had so many times before, how thankful I was to find such comfort in being in a home constructed a hundred years ago by a former soldier during the days when Fort Davis was active. The old house put its cool arms around me in summer, and now in the chilly prelude to winter, its snug warmth was a balm, soothing my troubled mind with its whispering sounds as the wind began to seep through the aged cracks.

The coffee finally swished and gurgled its way to an end, so I poured a cup and sank gratefully into my easy chair in the living room. Finally turning on a light, I looked distastefully at a legal pad and pen nearby. Forcing myself to pick them up, I fully intended to write a memo for the day to my employees at the hotel and restaurant. My faithful Jesse would come see about me if I didn't show up for work at six, and I thought it would be easier to write everything down, thereby saving energy by not having to talk. My right hand would not respond. My mind, in panic, said, "Write! Write! Write the story for your grandchildren!"

And as the wind rose, stirring the fall leaves, their musty sweet odor joined the air coming in around the tall narrow windows by my chair. A light tapping of sleet on the window panes announced the coming of an early storm, disturbing the quiet Indian summer morning. I began to write. . . .

I hope you will enjoy the coming tale of the ranger and the McKittricks. And, of course, the story of the cavalry in their quest to rid the area of the last of the renegades, and the sad retreat of the great Apaches from their homeland—God's country—the beautiful Davis Mountains of West Texas.

Joan Stocks Nobles
Fort Davis, Texas
Late Autumn 1990

ACKNOWLEDGMENTS

MY THANKS

—To Kay Edwards Hall, who first listened to my story, and then sent me a note to "Please write it for me." My editor, my dear friend—how on earth, Katie, have you been able to survive all of the misspelled words, bad typing, and even worse, the handwritten notes that would put a doctor to shame!

—To Elmer Kelton who, within a week of reading the first draft, wrote a six-page critique on how I could improve the story. A master of the written word—more, what better friend.

—To Nancy Jones, who first read parts of the story aloud to a group of friends and encouraged me to "Please finish your re-write." She has now taken it upon herself to put the complete book on audio tape. What a wonderful lady, whose voice puts an angel to shame.

—And to her husband, Asa, who has great knowledge of the West, horses, cavalry, and, I might add, next to my Daddy Stocks, is the greatest story teller I have ever heard.

—To delightful Vicki Snyder, whose doctor-husband is writing a book, and who told him, "David, you've got your work cut out for you if you can top this!"

—To my dear friends, June and Frank Cowden, who for over forty years have always supported me and encouraged me further in this exhausting task; to Dorothy and Clarence Scharbauer, Jr., who, after years of showing and riding their horses, now join me with the same enthusiasm as for their great Thoroughbred, Alysheba; to my college roommate, Mary Lou Danahy, who gracefully endured the smells of the stable in school. She said of my story, "It's beautiful." To Locke Sue Bisset, who came daily to read my first attempts, and didn't want me to change a thing. To Midland's English teacher emeritus, Dorothy Perkins, whose subtle changes of just one word made such a difference. To my lawyer, Ted Kerr, who, as a snotty-nose kid made my teenage life a terror; he insisted I get a copyright immediately. To Ann Enloe, a lovely lady who has always found the time to see and hear with me the beauty that surrounds us. To Barry Scobee, whose wonderful book, *Fort Davis*, gave me the factual state of post-Civil War Fort Davis. And those at the Haley Library and History Center of Midland, Frances and Evetts Haley, Jr., and Pat McDaniel, for finding it fascinating and asking if the story could possibly be true!

—And to my family—my brother Banky, whose smile lights up the sky when he remembers our grandfather and who tells his stories much better than I; my sister Sarah, "It's wonderful, believe it"; my learned daughter, Jane, who wouldn't help me because, "I'd ruin it, Mother, you're doing fine by yourself"; and her husband, Jim Bob, who said, "It sure holds your interest; I don't want to stop reading until I'm finished"' my son Joe's wife, Kathy, who said, "Gran, it's great! Hope it makes a movie"; And son Gerry, who smiled in wonder and chuckled, "Mom, it's really good!"

—And my special thanks to one of God's best men, my dear friend Bill Leftwich, author and artist bar none.

—And last but certainly not least, sincere appreciation for the kind words of Joyce Gibson Roach and Judy Alter and those at TCU Press who found my "faction" so enjoyable.

—All this kindness shown me has been overwhelming. Just know, dear ones, I have kept your written notes in a special place, your words within my heart. For, without you, I could never have done it.

—And now, what do you suppose my grandchildren will say?

God Bless.

FOREWORD

RUN WITH THE HORSES is a grand adventure tale full of bandits and horse thieves, cavalry and Indians. It's a tale of kidnapping and violence and suspense, and most of all, it's a tale of one remarkably brave and clever woman. It is the kind of story on which legends of the Old West were built.

But *Run with the Horses* shouldn't be dismissed as an old-fashioned western story, now hopelessly out of date and politically incorrect. It is, instead, literary folklore — a true story couched in the style and language of fiction.

The story is based on the family saga of the McKittricks, archetypal pioneers in the Big Bend country of West Texas' Davis Mountains, land that includes the Mexican borderlands. It is a region long distinct in lifestyle, language and prejudices.

In telling her family's legend, Joan Stocks Nobles uses stereotypical labels: Mexican bandits are cruel, frequently physically disfigured so that their appearances mirror their evil souls; Indians are stoic, leather-faced and bronze-skinned, and they are often called "braves"; a buffalo soldier sergeant speaks in the dialect of the former slave; even the lone Chinese character is a stereotype with slanted eyes. But Nobles writes also of gentle Mexican ranch hands who are devoted to the family and who are equally victims of the "bandidos." She is plainspoken about the presence of the U.S. cavalry, a mixed blessing, and she is forthright about classically heroic Texas Ranger John Revell as well as lesser *gringos*. The Apache Indians on these pages — Bird Man, High Cloud, and the chief White Cloud — are sympathetically depicted. The language is that of storytelling — young love spreads a warm glow, eyes mist with tenderness, hearts are moved.

Certainly, the language of *Run with the Horses* is not that of the 1990s, but the language, imagery and story are true to the time and place, true to border life in the post-Civil War days. It is in that light the book should be read and enjoyed as a grand adventure story. And, dear reader, if your heart isn't moved by the story, it's hard as stone.

Joyce Gibson Roach
Keller, Texas
Spring 1997

RUN WITH THE HORSES

1

Gran Carie

WHITE FROTH from the mouths of the runaway team floated as free as the bud of the cottonwood with each step of the straining animals. Carie rose from the seat of the wagon and slapped the reins against the mules' sides, urging them even faster. The clanking wheels raced the gritty, whirling dust-devil across the flats toward the rolling hills, beyond which the towering blue mountain obscured the horizon.

"Hi-i! Faster, Kit! Come on, Kate! Ay-yah-h!" The wagon bucked when the mules crossed a dry creekbed, almost toppling the wild, gray-headed woman. Regaining her balance, she continued to press the animals in their headlong rush upward, until she reached the crest of the hill.

"Whoa-a, ladies! Whoa!" she shouted.

Sitting down hard on the wooden seat, she braced her boots against the front footboard and pulled the reins with all of her remaining strength. As the labored mules came to a stop, Carie jumped from the wagon, almost falling to her knees, and staggered to the lead mule. Flinging her arms around the lathered neck, she laid her head on that of the brown jenny and with a trembling hand began to stroke the tawny muzzle.

"I'm sorry, Kit! I wouldn't hurt you and Kate for nothin'. I just went plumb crazy. I hate Carrasco, damn his worthless hide! I HATE him, just as much as he hates me!"

Raising her head, Carie looked directly into the soft brown eye of the mule, speaking as though the animal understood every word she said, "Oh, Kit, I've never hated anybody in my life" and, giving in to the terrifying emotion, laid her head again on Kit's cheek and sobbed as though her heart would break.

Tears mingled with the droplets of sweat on the mule's neck, and as her sobs lessened and fell into the rhythm of the heaving sides of the animal, she became aware of the salty, earthy taste of dust coating her lips.

Carie stepped back and walked to Kit's patiently standing partner and, patting her forehead, said, "Good girl, Kate, good girl." The mule answered by shaking its head, rubbing it against Carie's doeskin shirt, bringing a fleeting smile to the woman's weathered face. With labored steps Carie moved to the shade of a nearby oak and leaned against the rough bark of its huge trunk. She crumpled to sit on the grass, cross-legged.

Momentarily yielding to the shock of the last hour, Carie's trembling hands grasped the braided leather string that held her hat. Pulling it from her neck, she laid the battered beaver by her side. In doing so, her eyes caught sight of the bloodstained paper poking out of the pocket of her riding skirt. Slowly she pulled out the crumpled letter, unfolded it, and again read the words written in her husband's hand.

"Carie, love," it said, "this is to let you know that Billy Frank and I are being held captive by Chango Gomez in Rustler's Cave. This letter will be delivered to Carrasco de Monseis along with the finger they have cut from my right hand. This is a warning, Carie, that you are to do exactly what Señor de Monseis tells you, which is to round up as many of the horses as you can find and within a week's time take them to Gomez's *estancia*, west of Presidio. That's all the time that you have. Each day that you delay, Señor Gomez will cut off another finger of my right hand and send it to Carrasco. If this is not enough, they say they will beat Billy Frank with my own quirt.

"Let me reassure you that they have not harmed us, so far, other than the minor problem with my finger, which I don't want you to worry about. That's all that has happened to us. However, I beg you, my Gran Carie, do not do anything other than what you have been asked to do. Hopefully, we'll all be together in a week's time.

"Our hearts are with you, Lea, and the children."

Your Will

Her eyes continued to stare unseeingly at the letter, as her thoughts returned to the events of the morning. She had dreaded to leave the peaceful little canyon that held the family's adobe home, nestled in a small grove of live oak. She had hesitated as she looked back one last time at the wooden barn and picket corrals and heard the merry laughter of her grandchildren as they went about their chores. Her heart lifted, as it always did, when she saw the horses eating the fresh prairie hay. Her son's wife, Lea, had broken the reverie by walking out onto the porch. "Carie, sure you don't want me to go with you?"

"No, Lea," she said, smiling at the tall, beautiful woman, immaculate in a pretty calico dress and white starched apron bright as the morning sun. "You best stay with the kids. Fort Davis is no place for any of you. B'sides, no one will pay any mind to me!"

Lea chuckled and shook her head at the buckskin-clad little figure, beaver hat pulled down to her eyes and over a long gray braid tied this early morning with twine string from a flour sack.

Carie clucked to the mules and the wagon moved away. "Fort Davis is a cesspool!" she said in parting.

In that year of our Lord, 1866, Fort Davis lay desolate in the crisp autumn air, a disgrace to the serene beauty that surrounded it. The simple pine shacks with roofs of stretched tarpaulin had been built in a box canyon, its walls formed by an ancient volcano's lava rising from a fiery crater and then cooling to form a mouth of deep red, snaggled stone. The shacks had been built by troops of the Eighth United States Mounted Infantry in 1854, followed in the next three years by more substantial houses of pine and a sprinkling of adobe huts. This opened the way for white settlers and industrious Mexicans to settle in this land of high mountains, blessed with oak for their fires, cool spring-fed creeks, rich grasses, and a paradise of wildlife for their bellies. But it all came to a halt on April 13, 1861, when the U.S. Cavalry passed the Confederate cavalry in "salute"

4

by the banks of La Limpia. The Rebels didn't stay long; just a year later they decided it was wiser to fight the Yankees than the fierce Mescalero Apache. Their departure left the fort wide open for the Indians to pillage and burn. The less stalwart inhabitants drifted away, along with the post's trader, to seek shelter near the Rio Bravo, or farther west to El Paso del Norte. During the next five years, what had been one of America's most beautiful fort locations and a safe haven for weary travelers — east or west, north or south — became a virtual ghost town, its pine shacks empty, tarp roofs blown away by the cold northers, the adobe *salas* burned and desolate. These doors were now open only to the lowest of mankind — a combination of castoffs and deserters from both armies, Mexican bandidos, and renegade Indians banished from the Comanche and Apache tribes that had for centuries held these mountains. Fugitive marauders living in filth, drinking, killing, preying on hapless travelers, and ravaging the countryside of its wildlife. Stealing cattle, sheep, horses, vegetable crops, and grain from the few remaining settlers, whether Anglo, Mexican or Indian, and fouling their water with pestilence. A corrupt mercenary, one Carrasco de Monseis, had taken over the sutler's trading post and thus held a certain power over the area.

Carie drove the team toward the fort ruins and entered the rock-walled box canyon that held the fort. "A cesspool," she said again, as the stench of an open latrine made her gasp. The smell was made worse by the sight of Carrasco's large frame leaning in the doorway on the broken-down porch of the store, but she drove on and stopped the mules directly in front of the dilapidated building. *Probably hasn't washed in weeks,* she thought, looking at Carrasco's pock-marked face twisted in a grotesque smile, his puffy fat hands patting his protruding stomach.

"Come in, come in, Señora! I was just going to ride out to see you. You have spared me a hot ride in the sun. Come," he said, as he reached to open the sagging door, "I have something to show you!"

"Be right in," she said as she pulled the wagon's hand brake, deftly tied the reins around it, and stepped down. Rudely, Carrasco preceded her into the darkened, shuttered store.

"Tell your *gentes bajas* I need some flour and beans," Carie called out to his departing back as she reluctantly followed him inside. A new stench — a mixture of spoiled food, soured mash, and smoke — assaulted her. She hesitated, allowing her eyes to become accustomed to the half-light, and surveyed the room. It was a jumble of barrels containing tobacco, flour, beans, coffee, salted pork, and dried corn. The sagging wall shelves held assorted used, dirty clothing, worn hats, several army-issue rifles, and a couple of six-shooters. Crates stacked on the greasy, dirty floor held boxes marked "cartridges." In the center of the room stood a small pot-bellied stove, a round table, and a few dilapidated chairs. Carrasco was sprawled in one of them, his bloated, dissipated body spilling out among its wooden stiles. As Carie's sharp eyes focused, it was his leering, yellowed eyes reflecting the only stream of light coming from the open door that stopped Carie's survey of the room. *Looks like a damn panther after a kill,* she thought.

"I have something I want for you to read," Carrasco sneered, tossing a folded paper onto the table.

Carie moved toward the table and immediately spotted the bold lettering on the paper: "Carie McKittrick."

As she read the note, Carie gasped with outrage and

despair; it took all the will power she could muster to remain standing. Carrasco, however, was not finished with his torment. He tossed a bloodied bandana onto the table where it landed with a thud. The odor of decaying flesh challenged the stink of the room. She raised her eyes from the letter to meet Carrasco's cold ferret-like eyes as he announced, "Señor Will's finger, Señora," he smirked. "You want to see?"

No longer able to control the shock to her mind and body, her stomach knotted, and she clamped her eyes shut, fighting the awful nausea she felt. She grasped at the table for support.

Carrasco continued to smile contemptuously at the distraught woman.

Struggling to regain her composure, Carie raised her head, and through clenched teeth, muttered bitterly, "Why? Why would you do such a thing? What do you want? What will it take to get my men home?"

"Now, that's more like it, Señora Gra-awn Carie," as he drawled out her husband's pet name for her, "I have waited almost ten years for this day. The day I could pay you back for allowing the disease of the smallpox to take away my handsome face!"

Carie stared back at the man in utter incredulity. "But I doctored you, Carrasco, I tended you the same as everyone else!"

"Ah, you did," he said, looking at her with such hate that she stepped back. "But you left me and went to the Indio that the old one brought in, and you never came back! So now," he said, his eyes narrowing, "I want the horses that you have kept hidden during the war. The Bluecoats need horses to run the hostiles away to the reservations, and they pay *mucho dinero!* A small enough payment, Señora, for what you have done to me!"

"But High Cloud was only a little boy, Carrasco! I couldn't leave him!" Carie's voice rose, her mind desperately searching for words to mask the fear and loathing. "I don't have many horses and only four mules!"

The man's face became as hard as stone. "I will not argue with you. In a week's time, as the letter says, you deliver the horses to our good friend Gomez, and he will then send your men home. If you do not, they will die. . .ver-r-ry slow!"

"You're a madman!" she raged, "I can't get those horses in a week! Why, they're scattered all over, from the mountains to the flats!"

"Well, you'd just better do it in a week, because for every day you delay, we'll cut off another finger from Señor Will's hand! In a few days he will be just as big a cripple as your son." As an afterthought, Carrasco added with a chuckle, "Ah, the handsome Billy Frank. Gomez will have much fun whipping him with his own father's quirt!"

Anxiously, Carie closed her eyes briefly and swallowed, choking back the bile rising in her throat. She whispered, "You can't mean what you say!"

"Oh, *pero*, Señora, we do-oo-oo," he mimicked.

Sensing that the conversation was only getting worse, Carie made a quick decision. "Look, I'll make a deal with you. How many horses do you want?"

Carrasco, thinking he'd made his point and won, pressed his advantage. "Oh, a hundred of the best might be enough."

Looking at him in amazement, she screamed in shocked protest, "I don't have a hundred horses! I have only nineteen horses and two pair of mules. You know that! Will and Billy Frank took the rest when they went to Mexico to buy cattle!"

"I must have a hundred." Carrasco grinned, showing his yellowed teeth.

"And I have told you I have only nineteen, counting the mares and a few colts." Hesitantly, she added, "Maybe I can get a few more from the outlying ranches. But how can I? They lie in a hundred-mile radius and, with only the girls to help me, there's no way I can come near getting that many horses in a week's time."

"Don't try to fool me, Señora. Those girls can ride as good as you." The chair groaned as he rose to his full six-foot height. "But to show you how fair I am, I will agree to fifty horses and give you ten days." The man extended his beefy hand to shake hers. Carie's black-rimmed gray eyes flashed, and her lips curled in distaste, "Ten days, Señor de Monseis."

The staccato sound of her boots drowned out his mocking laughter as she ran from the store, jumped into the wagon and sped from the hated place. Her mind raced as she urged the mules across the mesa. "I must have a plan . . . I must have a plan!" she repeated as the wagon's iron wheel rims bounced across the clumpy grass and rocks. So intent was she that she took no note of a herd of antelope darting ahead of her, startled by the sight and sound of the wagon. She was oblivious, too, to the turkey buzzards circling above the swirling dust left in her wake and to the mother hawk's piercing protest from the nest she guarded in the oak tree where Carie had stopped to rest.

The germ of a plan formed in Carie's mind. Her hands no longer shaking, she reached into her pocket and pulled out the knotted, bloodstained bandana. Placing it tenderly on the ground beside her, she selected a sharp, flat rock and began to dig savagely into the ground. The rocky soil did not easily yield, and before she was satisfied that the hole was deep enough, the tender skin around her fingers was bloody. Therefore, when she picked up her husband's bandana, her own blood mingled with that on the neckpiece. Placing the sacred object into its small grave, she carefully covered it with dirt. She piled rocks on top until they were almost a foot high and equally that in diameter. Only when she was certain that predators could not disturb the grave did she arise and walk to her mules. With her jaw set in a hard line, and with agility that defied her fifty-nine years, Carie climbed into the wagon and headed home.

The team stopped in front of the house and, not bothering to tether them, Carie made her way hastily through the door. It opened to a sparsely furnished kitchen whose focal point was a huge, wood-burning cast-iron stove. Smells of coffee and simmering beans mingled with that of freshly baked loaves cooling on the sideboard. The long table was covered with brightly colored oilcloth, and ten chairs were in place around it. Carie thought how different were the sights and smells here from those in the room she had left just an hour before. Lea entered through an adjoining door that led to the family's sleeping porch. "Heard you drive up. Let me help you with the supplies."

Carie started, looking into the woman's face that spoke only kindness. "No, Lea. There are no supplies. Pour us some coffee and sit down with me. I have something I need to tell you."

With a questioning look, Lea did as she was bidden, and not a word was spoken until the two women were seated and facing each other across the table.

Carie took a long swallow of hot coffee, then raised her tired eyes to those patiently waiting.

"Gomez has Billy Frank and Will held prisoner at Rustler's Cave," she blurted out, thinking that the best way to tell her is to get it over with. Trying not to let the sight of her daughter-in-law's stricken face interfere with the telling of the horror, Carie's voice managed to spill forth every word that she and Carrasco had said. By the time Carie paused for breath, Lea was sobbing inconsolably into her apron. Carie put her arms around the shoulders of the younger woman. "There, there, Lea," she said quietly to the wife of her beloved son, "We'll get them back." With her face set in grim lines, Carie began to tell Lea of the plan.

"We'll send Missy to Bird Man to get the mares, Meri to High Cloud for the geldings and Willie to the Jones Ranch. . . ." She got no farther. Lea's tear-stained face came up with a start, eyes flashing with anger.

"Not my children!" she cried, "You'll not use my children!" her voice rising, "Let those sorry cut-throats have the damned horses! I don't care about the horses! They said they'd let the men go when they get the horses!"

"We have no choice, Lea, we all have to have a part in this, and there's no time to spare. Help is too far away. It would take too long even to try and go for help," Carie replied, trying to calm the distraught young mother. She reached to pat Lea's shoulder, but Lea jerked her arm away and pulled back in astonishment.

"Carie, you're crazy! You must be crazy!"

The conflict was more than Carie's mind and body could take, and she sank into a chair by Lea's side and, with her elbows on the table, buried her face in her hands. Speaking more to the table than to Lea she said, "They'll kill us all, anyway."

Silence filled the kitchen, neither woman moving

until at last, Lea's hand reached to cup Carie's chin and, raising it so their eyes met. "You're saying that they'll kill Billy Frank and Will anyway, horses or no?"

"Yes, Lea, they'll kill 'em. And they'll find us and kill us, too," she said with conviction. "They can't afford to let anyone know what they've done. The troops will soon be coming back to activate the fort, and the first people they'll ask after will be Will and Billy Frank McKittrick."

Lea's brown eyes expressed understanding and reluctant acceptance of what had to be. "I'll go call the kids and old Feliz," she said, and headed for the door.

"You plan for us to leave soon?"

"Real soon," was the reply.

Moments later, the clang of the triangle as Lea struck the metal bar against it brought Carie abruptly to her feet. With determination set in the lines of her weathered face, Carie was pouring coffee into her cup when her grandchildren burst into the room.

"What'd ya bring us from town, Gran Carie?" yelled Missy.

"Whatever it is," smiled Meri, grabbing her little sister around the mouth to muffle her screeching, "the flour'd better not have weevils in it this time. Last time, Mama stayed mad for a week."

"I'll help you unload," came the practical voice of their brother Willie.

No three children could be more different, thought Carie as she silently surveyed the McKittrick siblings.

Meredith, the eldest, blossoming into womanhood at seventeen, had the tall, stately figure of her mother. Her brown hair and eyes evoked thoughts of the blacktail doe, for she was a dreamer, always seeing the beauty of every living thing around her. "Meri" was certainly a most appropriate nickname, because humans and animals alike responded to the warmth of her sweet nature.

William Franklin McKittrick, III, had been granted the dark good looks of his father, but at nine, rather than the slim build of Billy Frank, his body was building to that of a mighty oak. Will must have looked like this when he was a youngster, thought Carie, but it's almost sad. Willie's never been a little boy. He's been the man of the family ever since his pa and grandpa went away to war.

Then there was Missy. It was Missy who made Carie's eyes soften when she beheld those of the twelve-year-old. Melissa McKittrick was the reincarnation of her grandmother. Small for her age, Missy had a mop of unruly light brown hair pulled back from her square, freckled face into a single long, thick braid. But it was her eyes that mesmerized anyone seeing Missy for the first time. Gray, lined in black, with heavy double lashes, they were pools of wonder sparkling with intelligence.

It was those very eyes now flashing in anger at her sister that brought Carie's thoughts back to the present — almost unbearable — task of dealing with them.

"Let go of me, dammit!" sang out Missy, breaking away from her sister.

"That's enough, Missy," Carie said quietly, "we have enough to do without you hollering at one another. And don't swear."

With her eyes focused on the floor, and brutally, as she had done with their mother, Carie continued in a grave voice, "Your pa and Grandpa Will were captured by Chango Gomez and his gang as they were coming back from the river. I'm guessing, but I figure our drovers were either killed or run off, and our cattle were stolen before our men could do anything about it.

Carrasco told me this morning that he wants a ransom of fifty horses for their release."

Carie raised her head and stared into the faces filled with shock. With all the strength of conviction within her small frame, she spoke in a voice husky with emotion. "They'll not have Grandpa Will, they'll not have your pa, and they'll not have our horses."

Ignoring the pain and disbelief she saw in the faces of her loved ones, and ignoring her own pain and fear, Carie continued, "Carrasco doesn't know we have over two hundred and fifty head of horses, counting the mares and colts, but, as I said, he's not going to get a single one of them. Those horses were protected and kept all those years when Will and Billy Frank were fightin' the war. While we stayed here, hid and raised the horses, your grandpa and pa saved their money and their mustering-out pay to buy more cattle. Cattle," she hissed, "taken first by the Unionists and then by the Confederates. Now our horses mean a new start in life — for all of us. And neither Carrasco nor his flunky Chango Gomez are going take 'em away from us! And what's more, they're sure as hell not going to have Will nor Billy Frank!"

Carie opened her arms wide, and her voice trembled as she told them, "Early this morning before I left for town, old Feliz told me his bones hurt; thinks a norther is coming in, and by the look of the sky, he's right. And that's going to help us. Now, let's all sit, pull ourselves together and try to eat a bite while I tell you how we're going to pull this off. We all have to work together. You'll each have your own part in this, and I don't want any misunderstanding from anybody about it."

Carie's legs finally gave way, and she sat down hard into her chair. But her face was still unshakeable with resolve as she watched the tears trickle down the cheeks of the listening youngsters.

Willie was the first to recover. "Gran Carie, why not just give them the horses?"

"Willie, I would, if I thought that would be enough. But for cut-throats like that bunch, it's not. Those horses are worth their weight in gold, and gold means greed."

Lea's voice broke in, "Don't you remember your pa telling us how many horses and mules were killed during the Civil War? Ten times more than all the human lives that were lost. And think of all the settlers that will be needing good breeding stock, as well as mules for their plows!"

Carie looked gratefully at her daughter-in-law as the youngsters' faces changed to excitement. They closed in around her, pelting her with questions. "Whoa, now," she said, smiling at the eager kids. "Get some of your ma's good stew and beans into your bellies; it's goin' to be a while before any of us will again have any hot food."

Her grandchildren's minds now turned to the excitement of the coming adventure. They filled their plates and began to eat with gusto. Thank the good Lord, Lea and I pulled that off, she thought, seeing the same relief reflected in Lea's face. Then, choosing her words carefully, Carie unfolded the plan.

"Missy will be the first to leave. She'll ride Skye's Son and take Boots north across Limpia Creek, on up into the mountains to the Bird Man's cave. With his help, she'll get the mares and colts."

Lea protested, "I think someone should go with her! Carie, she's only twelve years old!"

"Lea," said Carie, "she must do her part, and she's

the only one besides me who can ride the stallion, you know that. Boots will take care of her, and Skye's Son loves her. They'll be just fine, and the rest of us will be decoys."

Missy was proud that her grandmother had picked her first. She said with great importance, "I can do it, Gran Carie, and all by myself, too."

"Now Meri, you take Stretch; he can outrun anything on the ranch. You'll take the six geldings and go down Limpia Creek for five miles — and stay in the creek-bed — you'll meet Dry Canyon, on up to Wild Rose Pass, and then on to High Cloud's place by the bluff. With his help you can gather all the geldings he's been breaking for us and bring them around the mountains to meet Missy and me at San Martine Springs."

Willie, looking worried, spoke up, "Well, what do I do, Gran Carie?"

"As I said, Willie, you'll have a special part in this, too. Your mama and I will take you in the wagon, with Chance tied to the back of it, and head for Barrel Springs. When we get to the point where the road forks, you and your mama will go on to the springs, and I'll take ol' Hammer and go up through H-O Canyon to help Missy." The little fellow looked relieved, so Carie continued. "You'll drive on to the springs where you'll have a little 'accident' with the wagon and rest there for the night. Come first light, you'll take my horse and ride like hell to the Jones Ranch to tell them what's happened. Your mama will go on to Adobe Wells and try to find us some more help."

Carie turned to the girls, "We should be able to get to Salt Flat with the horses in three days' time. There'll be soldiers at the Salt Outpost that will help us." Her face crinkled into a wide grin as she added, "I think I can persuade them, especially when I offer them a hundred McKittrick horses for the army when we get our men free!"

All three smiled broadly at their grandmother, and Missy whooped with glee, "We can do it! I know we can do it!"

"We'll be only a day away from you, Lea," Carie said as she looked into Lea's sad brown eyes, "and from there, we'll go on to free our menfolk! Should be well under the time Carrasco granted me. Well, what d'ya think? Ever'body understand what we're goin' to do?"

"Yes, Carie, and now I do feel it will work. I pray it will," said Lea.

"Well, let's get moving," Carie announced, "get your saddlebags filled with biscuits and hardtack. Oh, and pack plenty of shells, while your mama checks your guns."

Carie jumped up, drained the last of her coffee and, with boots and spurs ringing against the hardwood floors, went out the back door, calling, "Feliz! *Pronto!* Feliz! *Andale, ándale!*"

An aged Mexican emerged from the barn. *"Sí, Patrona?"*

"Pronto, compadre, bring Skye's Son," she commanded.

The old Mexican didn't question when he saw her face. He turned back into the barn and brought out a beautiful, sleek Thoroughbred, solid black except for one white spot on his forehead. When the horse's soft brown eyes saw the woman before him, he raised his graceful neck and nickered loudly, as though he sensed something wrong and wanted to tell her that he would help, too.

"Put only a neck rope and surcingle on him, Feliz.

17

Also, let's bind his feet with rawhide. I don't want any-one to be able to track him or figure out where he's going. Now, let me tell you what has happened."

As she helped Feliz bind the horse's feet, Carie again related the events of the morning. Then she turned toward the house and called out, "Don't forget your canteens and slickers! And wear your brush jackets!"

As she spoke the last word, Missy came tearing out the back door, "We've already got 'em!" She came toward Carie, running across the yard to get on the horse. Carie caught the child by the shoulders to stop her, then laced her fingers together and bent over. Missy stepped into her grandmother's cupped hands to mount the great horse that towered over her.

"Up you go, child. Now, listen to me, Melissa. You must be clear as to what you are to do." Missy's mouth dropped open when her grandmother called her by her "real" name.

"Hand me your rifle." Carie put the weapon in the loop of the surcingle, and whistled for Boots. She patted the dog and lifted him to settle in front of the child.

"Hold him tight, Missy, and carry him in your saddle until after you've crossed Limpia; we don't want to leave any tracks. It's rocky on the north side, and there you can put Boots down and take the rawhide from the horse's feet. That is, if it's not already worn off."

Lea stood silently, tying the saddlebags to the back of the surcingle, as Carie continued, "Don't tarry, Missy! I don't think you can get to the cave by nightfall, but try your best. Skye's Son is fresh, so don't spare him — he'll be all right. But if you get tired and sleepy, hook your arms through the neck rein and lay your head on his neck and rest. He'll keep going because he'll know he's going to get his mares."

With that, Missy leaned from her mount to give her mother a hug. Smiling at both women and holding the dog tightly, Missy turned the great Thoroughbred north toward the high mountains and spurred him into a lope.

They all watched the little girl until she topped the ridge and dropped from sight.

Carie turned to the old Mexican. "Feliz, please get Stretch for Meri. Then go down to the pen on the creek and halter the geldings and tie them together. All but Crook. Leave him in the pen.

Feliz said, "Sí, Patrona, but why not take Crook?"

"I'll explain later," she replied.

Feliz shook his head and trotted off.

Lea said to her daughter, "Meredith, be careful. Please, be careful!"

"Don't you worry, Mama. Stretch can outrun any horse in the country. Just think of all the races that I've won against all the kids around here and, for that matter, all the men, too! There's nobody can catch Stretch!" Then she, too, hugged her mother, turned and ran toward the pen, holding her rifle in one hand, her saddlebags in the other.

"Meri," Carie yelled after her, "if you're spotted by anyone, just drop the rope on those geldings and run!"

Willie came from the barn leading Carie's small gray gelding. Tearing her eyes from Meri's departing figure, Carie turned to Willie and said, "Now, grandson, it's your turn! Let me have Chance and you go in the barn and get some of Feliz's oldest clothes and a sombrero for Gran to put on. And, Lea, you go back in the house and find some clothes of mine for Willie to put on. If anyone sees you, we want them to think it's me sitting beside you."

The beautiful Lea smiled and said, "I've already figured out what you had in mind," and she pulled out an old, battered hat, a brush jacket and some warm, leather leggings.

Willie reappeared with an old sombrero, poncho, and well-worn pants. As Carie hastily put them on, Lea helped dress Willie. When all was straight, all three laughed.

"My goodness, William Franklin McKittrick the Third, you're as big as I am! Just keep that hat pulled down or that black hair will be a dead give-away!"

Willie beamed, "Don't worry none, Gran, I'll turn my collar up!"

Carie sobered, "Now, let's take the harness off Kit and Kate and hitch up Hit and Hammer. Kit and Kate are both tired; I ran 'em too hard and they can't go much further. Willie, when we get the harness off, take 'em down to the creek and turn 'em loose on the other side. They'll head south and, with luck, their tracks will lead Carrasco and his bunch on a false trail. I know Carrasco will probably come out here by mornin' to see what we're doin', and maybe — just maybe — they'll follow the mules' tracks. There's no way they could find those mules — those two will stay ahead of them for a half a mile and never let that bunch get near 'em. Also, Crook is so damned mean, Meri needn't be worryin' about him."

Even though her face was strained with worry, Lea couldn't help but chuckle. "I'm thankful that you did· leave him, Carie. Will wanted you to get rid of him a long time ago."

Carie went into the corral and brought out two huge red mules. The two women harnessed and hitched them to the wagon. As the young boy came running back from the creek, Carie said, "Willie, tie Chance to the tailgate and climb on. You drive, Lea; and Willie, you sit beside her. I'll crawl into the wagon bed and pull a tarp over me, 'cause I need a little rest and some time to think. Let's hurry, now, so we can be off!"

"Señorita Meri, she's gone," said Feliz as he came trotting toward them.

"That's fine, Feliz," replied Carie. "Now listen carefully. Do you have Crook in the pen?"

"*Sí, Patrona.*"

"Feliz, I think you know what we must do. Those sorry hombres from town will probably be here by daybreak. You've got to buy us some time. But whatever you do, don't let them see you or they'll kill you, same as us! So keep your horse saddled and hide him good. Just stall 'em any way you can, but don't take any chances, understand?"

With devilish glee, Feliz answered, "I'll do as you say, *Patrona*. I'll make them think you have gone south, and will take great joy at Carrasco's meeting the wild one!"

Then, sobering, he removed his hat and placed it reverently against his chest. "*Vaya con Dios, Patrona.* God go with you, *mi compadre,* Willie, and Señora Lea. Bring Señor Will and Billy Frank home."

Willie leaned over the side of the wagon and hugged the faithful old man's neck.

Lea slapped the reins. "Giddy-yap!" She circled the team into the western sun.

Carie waved at Feliz, rolled the leggings for a pillow and then laid down in the wagon-bed, pulling the canvas over herself. As she bounced along, her thoughts went back — forty years — to her first sight of William Franklin McKittrick.

ᐱᐯᐱ

Carolina McDonald was eighteen years old when she first saw him in the summer of 1826. He rode through the big double doors of her father's livery stable in Knoxville, Tennessee, as she was lugging a pitchfork full of hay to feed the horses in the stalls. She looked up at the giant black horse ridden by the equally giant man, dressed totally in black, from hat to boots. Startled, she said, "Mercy! You look like the devil himself!"

Rugged handsomeness with merry black eyes looked down at her, and the man threw back his head and laughed, "'Tis me! 'Tis the devil, or will be, if I don't get some feed and water for my horse, right now!" Observing the tiny figure, he said, "You're a mite small to feed and care for the likes of Skye. Where's the men around here?"

Eyes like smoked crystal met his and she retorted angrily, "I take care of the horses. And whoever would think to name a horse after the sky? The sky's blue, y' know!"

Feigning shock, the man said, "You? You take care of the horses? Why, you're no bigger than my hand! And, as for my horse, he takes me to the sky and beyond!"

She looked up at him squarely and said, "I'm five feet three, but Pa says I do the work of a man six feet three. As for your horse, he does look like the night sky with that white star in his forehead."

The dark man threw back his head and laughed at the expression of admiration on the square little face. Looking deep into her gray eyes, he said, "Well, I might say, you may be small, but from the looks of your eyes, you can do anything." He dismounted and handed the reins to Carie.

The man's bold stare caused Carie's heart to beat frantically, and she felt her knees going weak. A smile heretofore seen by no man darted across her face as his husky voice spread over her like a caress. "Think you can handle him, do you?"

"Him and you, too, if need be," was her flippant reply.

From the back of the stable came a short, burly, bald-headed man with his hand outstretched. "Hayes McDonald, sir," he said, as he shook the stranger's hand. "Best stable in this part of the country. And who might thou be?"

"Will McKittrick is the name, sir."

"Well, I'm glad to meet thee. Where are you headed, sir, or do you plan to stay with us for a spell?"

Will's grin broadened. "Glad to be here, but no, I won't be staying in these parts. In three days' time I'm leaving on the ship *Good Hope*, bound for Galveston. That's in Texas, you know."

"Lordy be," McDonald replied, "You going to Texas? Why, that's no place for anything but Indians!"

Shaking his head, Will answered with a smile, "Oh, no, Texas is real civilized. There's people going there every day. I know, for I've been there for two years. Already have a hauling business, and I raise horses and mules on a little spread north of the port."

McDonald, admiring the black horse, said, "Well, I'll say one thing for you, sir, you should do well with this fellow. I've never seen such a beautiful piece of horse-flesh. A true Thoroughbred, 'tis my way of thinking."

"Aye, he is that!" boasted Will. "Bought him off the ship from Ireland while I was in Boston just four weeks ago. Fellow that sold him to me said he was unmanage-able." His eyes twinkled as he laughed again. "All the proud black needed was a strong and steady hand."

Both turned to see the young girl lovingly rubbing

the horse's neck and shoulders, and cooing to him in a soft voice, "Oh, my beauty, such strength in those shoulders and muscles, and what fine legs you have! You must run like the wind!" The horse turned his head and gently nuzzled against her chest.

"My Gawd," said McKittrick, "I do believe she has hypnotized my horse! I never saw a woman that had such a touch with horses. Skye usually won't let anyone touch him 'cept me, and certainly not women. They're usually afraid of the big galoot!"

McDonald swelled with pride as he said, "That's my daughter, Carie. Her name's Carolina, but we call her Carie. Yes, she does have the touch; that's all she knows, for she's played with them in this stable since she was a baby. There's never been a horse that she has been afraid of, nor one that's been afraid of her. They know it, they feel it — they love her. Sometimes I think she's part horse — she can make them do anything!"

William McKittrick squinted his eyes at the girl with the sparkling eyes, the small but strong body, and said with wonder, "Aye, she is gran', 'tis Carie."

Three days later, when the vessel *Good Hope* left the port at Knoxville, Will and Skye, and Carie as well, were on their way to Texas. In the hold of the ship, in a stall next to the black stallion, was a dainty little gray Morgan mare with a bay filly colt by her side — Hayes McDonald's wedding gift to his precious only child and her new husband.

ᐯᐯᐯ

As Carie began to doze with the warmth of the tarp and the sway of the wagon, she thought, *Oh, Papa, I wonder if you'd have ever let me leave had you known what our life would be like. Seems like we've been strugglin' and fightin' someone or somethin' all our married life. It was pure hell when Will left Billy Frank and me to go help Sam Houston make Texas a state. But it was worse when they both left to fight for our country. To have to watch Lea work and worry, and the grandkids grow up too soon. And now this! Oh, Papa, I just know you're up there in God's heaven—please ask Him again for me to keep them safe and give me strength to rescue them. God knows, too, Papa, I'm so in fear of taking this terrible chance with all our lives, but I don't know what else I can do. I just know that I must use all of us to get back my Will and Billy Frank. Oh, Lord, please help me!*

The exhausted Carie drifted off into an uneasy sleep.

2

Missy

MISSY LOOKED BACK just once as she reached the high ridge that bordered the vast bowl-shaped mesa below her, encircled by low, rolling hills and sparsely sprinkled with oak and mountain cedar. Her eyes teared as she saw the wagon turning onto the road leading westward. Her heart hammered as she gripped the neck rope with her left hand and hugged Boots to her chest with her right, her body molded to the great stallion's back as if she and the horse were one.

Skye's Son, sensing his precious cargo's troubled spirit, cocked an ear back and slowed his gait to a walk. This brought Missy back to her task, and she clucked to the horse, urging him on.

"Boots," she said, choking back a sob, "we'll be at Limpia in just a little while, and then I'll put you down." Boots turned his head up at the sound of the girl's voice, not in the least concerned, for he had ridden in front of his mistress as a pup when his feet would become sore from the rocks or his body became tired from the many miles they had to travel. He, like the child, relaxed to the ease of the horse's stride as Skye's Son made his way carefully down the slope to the lush, winding valley that held the spring-fed Limpia.

The north wind had picked up by the time the three arrived at their first destination and crossed the shallow stream. Missy slid off the horse's back and turned to carefully lift the dog to the rocky bank. As she rubbed and slapped her cramped hands, the animals dropped their heads to drink the refreshing water. With circulation restored, she in turn went to her knees and, leaning, cupped her hands to drink of the cold, clear water. Brushing her hands against her leggings, she rose and awkwardly began to untie the rawhide from the horse's feet.

"Skye's Son," she said, as she struggled with the leather thongs, "I'm sure glad this rawhide is wet, for if it was dry I'd never have got it off! This must have come from that old twenty-point buck Gran Carie killed last winter just 'fore Christmas."

Looking up, as if she expected the horse to respond, she saw the magnificent black head rear back and ears point toward a tumbled-down pine shack on the creek bank a mile upstream. Boots, equally alert, stood as still as a stone, his yellow eyes trained on the same object as the horse's.

"Golly, gee!" she laughed, "whats the matter with you two? It's just the old sawmill where Gran Carie and Grandpa Will used to live." And, as she finally untied the last hoof, she straightened up and patted the shoulder of the horse, noticing the horse's eyes still trained on the old building. This brought memories of her home, her family, and her immediate task, and tears welled up in the child's eyes. Angrily wiping her nose on her sleeve, she clapped her hands and said, "Come on, Boots! Let's go, Skye's Son!" The horse responded by shaking his head, and the dog rushed to the girl, jumping to put his front paws on her chest, happily licking her face.

The frown on the little girl's face was erased and she laughed, digging her fingers into the dog's long hair at his collar and hugging his head next to her chest. "Good dog," she said happily, then pushed him away.

Catching the lead rope in her hand, she led the horse to a nearby boulder, crawled up on the rock and swung her body onto his broad back. Gripping the ring of the surcingle with her right hand, she lightly tapped her heels against the horse's sides, once again heading north. Glancing upward to the high Apache Mountains, she asked, "Do you think you can get us up there by dark, to where the colts and mares are?" The stallion responded by settling into an easy, mile-covering lope. This time, however, Missy could feel the purposeful power of his muscle-driven legs. As they steadily climbed, Boots following at their heels, the horse pricked up his ears, and his neck rose as if he could already see his mares.

MM

Two bronze bodies, naked save for the soft doeskin breechcloths they wore, faces streaked with vermilion, stepped from the shadows of the old sawmill and watched as the great horse carried the child away. "Go!" said one, "Tell our chief of the white child riding the black devil into our mountains." Without answering, the other quickly moved to his horse staked inside the dirt-floored shack. As he sprung onto the paint's back, the first man stepped to his side, a lone eagle feather in his black, braided hair fluttering in the chill breeze, and said, "I will follow the child. She goes to the Holy One."

As the one disappeared toward the highest of the peaks to the northwest, the other mounted his sturdy little unshod paint and silently followed Missy.

/\\/\\/\\

As the terrain became steeper, the black stallion slowed to a long, striding walk. With the biting wind in her face, Missy bent lower over the horse's neck and wrapped her arms through the neck rope. Using his head as a windbreak and his body to gather warmth, she felt almost comfortable. The lulling motion caused her to lay her head down against his neck, withers guiding him up the steep trail. His ironclad hooves rang out as they struck the rocky trail. Missy felt the soft caress of the silky mane against her cheek; she closed her eyes and fell peacefully asleep. The horse, with one ear cocked back listening to the child's breathing, moved cautiously among the rocks and brush of the mountainside. Sweat broke out on his sleek neck and his straining forelegs and flanks, but he never faltered, pushing continually onward. The dog, with his tongue keeping time to the beat of the horse's feet, panted as he struggled to follow.

What seemed but a few minutes was, in reality, almost an hour. Missy was jolted awake by the horse moving downward.

"Mercy, Skye's Son, where are we?" She blinked as she sat up. As if on cue, the horse stopped and turned his head toward her. Boots trotted to the horse's side and dropped to his belly, sides heaving from exertion. Rubbing her sleeve across her forehead, then shaking her head to clear it of the deep sleep, Missy became aware of the tall pines as they sighed in the cold wind. "Ooooh, we're already up to timberline," she said excitedly, "just about to go into Madiera Canyon! Only one more mountain to climb and we'll be at Bird Man's cave!"

She slid down from the horse and, picking up the collie and placing him across the horse's withers, said, "You ride now, Boots, for you're just plain tuckered out!" Turning the horse sideways and downhill, she scrambled onto his back and righted herself behind Boots. With his precious burden, Skye's Son again began to move at a faster pace, carefully picking his way down into the deep canyon.

By the time the horse, dog, and girl rounded the next high point, the sky had darkened to a muddy gray, and stinging sleet began to coat the trio, the mountain oak, juniper, and pinions with glistening ice. Missy looked across at the opposite canyon wall to an outcropping of rock. Wisps of smoke escaped from the cracks in the surface above. "We made it, Skye's Son! Look, Boots! Bird

Man's got a fire, which means food! Beans for me, grain for Skye, and maybe a bone with a little meat on it for you!" The dog barked in reply and sprang from his perch, and for the first time ran ahead of the horse and girl toward a stand of trees in the canyon floor. Missy sensed the increased excitement of the horse, but he continued to step gingerly among the rocks and brush until they reached the trees standing near a tranquil pond.

This time Missy didn't slide off but swung a leg over the animal's back and jumped down. She reached up, carefully drew the rifle from the surcingle, laid it on a rock, and began to remove the surcingle.

"Skye's Son," she said, speaking directly to the horse's head as though he could understand every word, "I'm gonna leave your neck rope on, so that tomorrow when you bring the mares and colts in to water, you'll be real easy to catch. That way, we'll not lose any time meetin' Gran Carie." Then, slapping him lightly on the flank she said, "Now, go find your family!"

Skye's Son turned slowly, rubbing his lathered head against her chest. Then he whirled, threw up both head and tail, and nickered. The echo bounced off the deep canyon wall so loudly that it sounded like a dozen horses answering. Even though the horse had already traveled with his burden over more than twenty miles of high mountains and deep canyons, he thundered away at a dead run.

Boots began to bark, reminding Missy where she was and what she had to do. Ruffling the dog's ears and patting him, Missy said, "Boots, did you find Bird Man? That smoke sure looks invitin'. My hands and feet feel

like they're froze plum' off! Let's go find that ol' man."
She retrieved her rifle, and the pair scurried happily up
the bluff, eager for the protection of the cave.

They found it deserted, but a cheerful fire was burning, and two Dutch ovens hung over a hot bed of coals.
A bedroll was laid out, and there were camp supplies,
saddle, blankets, a hand-pleated bosal, and several
rawhide satchels brimming full of golden kernel dried
corn. But no human being. This, however, did not alarm
Missy, and she ran to the fire, holding out her hands for
welcome warmth, rubbing them briskly together. "He's
probably just gone to check on something and will turn
up 'fore long. Come on, Boots, let's eat!"

With a long hook she lifted the lids off the two pots.
"Whoopee!" she hollered, "Beans and venison stew!"
Missy ladled two tin plates full, and the two friends hun-
grily gulped down their feast.

/\.\/\.\/\

The man finally moved from the fresh mound of dirt
and leaned his shovel against the nearest oak tree. He
still could not believe what he had just seen, nor would
he have believed that there was anyone within ten miles
of him, had it not been for the dog's first bark. He was
startled, for he had been intent on getting the last shovel
of dirt on the Indian's grave. When he heard the bark,
he stopped and stared at a kid riding bareback on the
most beautiful black horse he'd ever seen. The horse had
only a neck rope to guide him, and the kid was hanging
onto a sursingle with a rifle stuck in its side! He watched
silently as the unlikely trio came down from the top of

the mountain and stopped at the spring. The kid had talked to both horse and dog, and that was when he realized the horse was a stallion, which made the picture even harder to understand. By the time the black steed turned and raced alone down the canyon, nickering loud enough to wake the dead, the man was even more puzzled.

Had the child looked his way, he could have easily been seen, for he was a mere twenty feet from them, right in the line of sight. The man sighed and said to himself, "Gawd! That's a sight I'll never forget! Best to go find out what's goin' on," and he followed the trail leading to the cave.

Warmed by the fire and Bird Man's stew and beans, Missy lay peacefully on a blanket. Boots, gnawing on a bone provided by his mistress, had found a perfect spot beneath the saddle.

Boots saw him first, but never moved, just stayed beneath the saddle, his eyes locked onto the man. When Missy heard his footfall on the cave floor, she turned up, saying, "Bird Man, that venison—uh, who in the hell are you?" Missy jumped up and, grabbing her rifle, swung it toward the intruder in one smooth motion. "I asked who you are! Where did you come from? Where in the hell is Bird Man!" she screeched.

A haggard, bearded face with deep lines around tired brown eyes looked at the child blankly, then transformed as he smiled and said, "Listen, son, put down that peashooter and I'll be glad to tell you who I am." He reached out to take the gun from Missy's hands.

She, in turn, jerked the rifle even higher. "I wouldn't do that if I was you, mister, 'cause I might shoot you—

or, 'fore I did, Boots would be at your throat before you could blink an eye."

"If you mean that collie, well. . . ." Laughing, the man again reached for the gun. A low growl and the click of a hammer being pulled back were heard in the same instant. The man slowly pulled back his arm, sighed, and stepped back. Looking into the child's steely gray eyes, he slowly raised both hands above his head and solemnly said, "Okay, kid, you win. I surrender. Put the gun down and call off your dog."

Neither Missy nor Boots moved. Missy shouted, all in one breath, "I asked you first! What's your name? Where are you from? Where's Bird Man? And *I ain't no kid!*"

Mirth building within the stocky body finally exploded and he chuckled, "Well, I'll have to admit you *are* something, the way you ride a horse! The name's John Revell, Texas Ranger, headed to Fort Davis to keep the law at the Fort until the cavalry comes back to take it over." He got no further, because Missy went completely berserk.

"Johnny Reb, you say! I don't believe this! I can't wait to tell Gran Carie that I caught the Johnny Reb who shot Pa's leg off! I should kill you where you stand!" She gulped to get her breath. "If I'd of spied them gray trousers with them stripes 'neath that coat you're wearin', I'd of shot you *before* I asked any questions! You ain't no Ranger, you're just another cut-throat going to join that stinkin' de Monseis bunch, and do more killin'!"

John's smile instantly turned to a sorrowful frown. "Say, kid, I said Revell, not Reb, and, as far as I know, I may have shot someone in the leg, but I hope it wasn't your father." Wide shoulders slumped as he haltingly continued. "As for the old Indian, I found him when I came in here with my saddle and gear that your dog's guarding over there. About a mile back I had to shoot my horse when he stepped into a prairie dog hole and broke his leg. The Indian was dead—he'd been snakebit. I was buryin' him when you rode in."

Missy's expression mellowed as Revell told his tale, her rifle gradually sagging until it hung limply near the floor. Tears welled up in the shocked eyes and, as she had done at Limpia Creek, she rubbed her left sleeve against her nose. "Show me where you buried him, and be quick about it!"

John cocked his ear to hear the north wind whistling outside and in a consoling voice said, "I'm sorry about the poor man. Wouldn't want to see anybody die that way, but listen," pointing to the cave mouth, "there's no need to go back out there in the cold and sleet. I was just twenty feet from where you stopped your horse, under that first big oak." The sight of the furious little face and the ridiculous situation that he found himself in got the better of John Revell. "Now, calm down, kid, or I might have to wash your mouth out with soap!" and he laughed aloud.

Missy's tears turned hot with fury, and the rifle again went up. "Don't you talk to me that-a-way! And I ain't no kid! I'm a girl!" She yanked off her floppy hat and two long, brown braids fell almost to her waist.

It was John Revell's turn to be speechless. His hands dropped to his stomach as he burst out laughing until tears rolled down his cheeks.

Missy's face took on a deep red glow, and she chewed

on her lip, but her voice remained strong. "Just put your hands out, Johnny Reb, so's I can tie 'em, 'cause me and Boots need to get some sleep. The horses should be here by mid-mornin'. We've got to meet Gran Carie at San Martine Springs. Then see if you can tell her your yarn 'fore she shoots you!" The Ranger, still smiling at the pert little face, dutifully held out his fists and allowed Missy to bind them with the leather thongs she had taken from Skye's Son's feet. She then looked up at him with a sparkling smile and said sweetly, "Johnny Reb, you can have the horse blankets. Boots and me will take the bedroll. G'night! C'mon, Boots, let's get some sleep."

Boots trotted out from under the saddle and lay down next to Missy. After taking a couple of turns and snuggling next to the soft bundle of fur, Missy fell asleep cradling the rifle next to her body.

As the child's body became still, John raised his wrists to his mouth and, using his teeth, easily released himself from bondage. He picked up his canteen from where it lay near his saddle and poured some water onto a tin plate. Slipping his bandana from his neck, he dipped it into the cold water and scrubbed his grimy face and hands. Refreshed, he ladled a huge plateful of stew and beans onto the plate. He sat crosslegged on the dirt floor and hungrily began to eat, smiling all the while. *Don't know when I have laughed so hard,* he thought and, as if he was surprised at himself, *and I sure can't remember when I ever felt so good!*

After he had finished, he lifted the heavy pots from the fire and covered them. He scrubbed the three dirty plates with sand from the cave floor. Only when he was satisfied that all was well did he lay his almost six-foot body down on the cold blankets.

During the night, Missy cried out in her sleep. John Revell rose from his bed and crossed quickly to her side. Gently drawing the heavy quilt around her small shoulders, he patted the little girl and softly whispered, "Hush now, little one, everything's going to be all right."

The tiny woman-child sighed and relaxed into a deep sleep. The Ranger quietly returned to his cold blankets and lay down. Boots never moved, nor did his eyes ever leave the man.

As the first hint of sunrise appeared above the canyon rim, Missy awoke to Boots licking her face. She sat up quickly, rubbing her eyes. She uncurled and stretched like a kitten, blinking sleep from her eyes. There by the fire crouched Johnny Reb, stirring the bacon with hands still bound together. Missy's brow furrowed as she wondered how he could cook with his hands tied. But, oh, did it smell good! Pushing back the covers, she said, "Mornin'."

Missy noticed for the first time that the Ranger's light brown hair was almost as curly as his beard, and his rugged face was surely not unhandsome as he smiled. "Mornin', little lady, rest well? Rise and shine, our vittles are almost ready."

Forgetting her pleasant thoughts of the man, she glared with unreasoning fury, "Don't you be givin' me no orders around here. You're the one that's a pris'ner!" Jumping up, she grabbed her rifle and said, "C'mon, Boots, we gotta go wash up."

John grinned as he watched the feisty little girl and

her dog leave the cave. *Called me a pris'ner! Gawd, what a kid,* he thought, chuckling as he continued turning the pork. Minutes later, as he was lifting the heavy pan from the fire, there came a piercing scream. Dropping everything, he raced to the mouth of the cave, but was so shocked at the sight he beheld that he could move no further.

Missy was screaming, dancing first on one foot and then the other, waving the rifle above her head. "Get 'em, Boots! Get that son-of-a-gun! Boots, throw the viper—break his durn back!"

The dog was grasping the snake with his teeth. He would sling it away with a mighty snap of his head, then run to it, grab it again, shake it and sling it away again. He kept up the process, and Missy kept on hollering. Within minutes, the rattler no longer moved nor buzzed, and Missy ran to the dog standing over his trophy and flung her arms around his neck. "Good dog! Good dog! Blind old rattler that got Bird Man!"

She stood up, somewhat chagrined, and turned to the man standing at the mouth of the cave. "I'll say one thing for you, Johnny Reb, you did tell the truth about the snake, so I guess I can believe you about Bird Man." She gestured in the direction of the freshly-turned mound of earth at the foot of the great oak. "Poor old Bird Man, he didn't see very good, either, but Gran Carie still ain't gonna like hearin' he's dead. He was special 'cause he took such good care of the mares and colts." Then frowning, she waved her rifle at the high ridge above. "And the 'Paches will *really* be sad. They think of him as a Holy Man."

"What do you mean by 'Holy Man'?" the Ranger

asked frowning in puzzlement. Looking back at the man as if he were the dumbest person she'd ever seen, she saucily replied, "Because he was such a smart old codger! He could tell by the birds what kind of weather we'd be having — sometimes for a whole year! And he was good at doctorin', just like Gran Carie!"

"Oh," replied John, nodding his head. "I'm sure glad for your snake-killing dog." He smiled again. "Best get washed, breakfast is ready." Remembering that he had dropped the skillet, he quickly re-entered the cave. It was only then that Missy realized the Ranger's hands were untied. She just shook her head and hurried to the pond.

The two had just finished cleaning the tin plates and cups from their meal when the sound of thundering hoofbeats echoed through the canyon. John looked questioningly at Missy. "Now what's happening?"

"It's Skye's Son, bringing in the mares and colts!" Clapping her hands, she ran to the mouth of the cave.

"And which Indian is Skye's Son?"

Missy pointed down the canyon. "Skye's Son is no Indian," she replied impatiently, "He's Gran Carie's stallion that you saw me riding yesterday."

Completely forgetting any animosity she had felt for the man, Missy's freckled face was ecstatic. She looked up at the Ranger and shouted with glee. "Look! Oh, look, Johnny Reb, how big the colts have grown! Most are six months old and ready to be weaned!" Both stood transfixed as they beheld the graceful mares and colts in colors of black, brown, bay, sorrel, gray, paint, grulla, strawberry roan, and dun; and, wonder of wonders, every now and then there would be a long-eared mule colt, braying as it tried to keep pace with its mother as they raced to the spring.

"Well, hello, Alice," Missy said, pointing to a gray mare that had stopped to look up at them. "That ol' mare was the first colt Grandpa Will raised after they moved to Fort Davis. She's our 'lead mare.' Where she goes, the rest will follow. Oh, Alice, is that your black colt there by your side? It must be! Won't Grandpa Will be proud of you! And look, there's Delicious! See, Johnny Reb, the roan mare with the bald face? She has another fine, black baby!" Her little face was visited by a puzzled frown. "Now, how in the world did *that* happen?"

John was filled with delight as the little girl talked first to the horses and then to him. He didn't know which he was enjoying more—Missy's excitement or the awesome sight of more than two hundred horses.

"There comes Skye's Son!" And sure enough, the black stallion, with his outstretched neck lowered, herded the last of his remuda to crowd around the pond.

Boots began to bark, disturbing John's reverie, but Missy again caught his attention.

"Gran Carie! Gran Carie!" she shouted, waving toward the ridge across from them. "What a surprise! I didn't expect to see you until we got to San Martine Springs!" With a yelp, she darted down the bluff, the barking dog following at her heels. They rushed through the entire herd, not disturbing the animals one bit, while Missy spoke to each one as she passed. "Hello, Minnie, Pretty One!" And, "You're still too fat, Tightwad, but I'll forgive you 'cause of that bay colt. . . . Baby Doll, Pa will be home soon. He'll love seeing your filly!"

As Missy looked up at the figure high on the ridge, she waved and yelled, "Gran Carie! Aren't they just too pretty to be true?"

John, anxiously watching the girl, now turned his attention to the form slowly approaching her. To him the figure appeared to be a Mexican in poncho and sombrero, riding the largest red mule he had ever seen. *Ah, well, John Revell,* he thought, *one more outlandish person can't hurt you. Best go and meet the lady.* He slowly followed Missy but was careful to go around most of the mares and colts, for fear of being kicked.

John wondered what to expect with the newest arrival on this incredible scene. As he neared the approaching woman and Missy, now chattering away by her side, he removed his hat.

By way of introduction, Missy said, "This here's Johnny Reb, Gran Carie. He's my pris'ner that I was tellin' you about!"

"How do, Ma'am," John said, as he looked into eyes that almost jolted him backward. Steely gray, fringed in black, they reached into his very soul. Eyes that silently appraised the man inside and, finding goodness, sparkled in welcome.

"It's nice to meet you, Ranger. We heard you were coming weeks ago, but I never expected to find you out here," replied the husky voice. Carie stiffly dismounted and turned to grasp his hand in a firm grip. "Welcome, John Revell. I'm Carolina McDonald McKittrick — Carie to my friends." Finally smiling into John's dumbstruck face she said, "And I sure hope you'll be a friend, for what you've walked into here is another war — a fight to save my husband, my son, and my horses. Hope you can help us."

The Ranger, subdued by emotion, could only whisper in reply, "It's my job, ma'am, and of course I'll do everything I can."

"Good! Thank you." Now turning to Missy, she hugged the child. "You did well, Melissa."

Carie, leading the mule, moved through all of the herd, speaking softly and touching each animal until she reached the stallion. Laying her head against the black stallion's neck, she patted his shoulder and said, "Thanks, old friend."

Missy and John silently observed the strength and presence of the small woman. Missy broke the spell. "That's Gran Carie."

"Aye, that's a Gran Carie," John replied. The pair followed along behind Carie as she greeted her horses. Not another word was spoken until they reached the pond, when Carie turned to them.

"Hope you have some coffee and a good fire. The cold and sleet have left my old bones aching."

John jumped forward as she spoke, "You bet, ma'am, and there's plenty of beans and stew. Let me take your mule, and you and the kid go on up to where it's warm."

Missy's past good humor vanished, and she lashed out, "I keep tellin' you, I ain't no kid! Gimmee that mule, I'll take care of 'im." She grabbed for Hammer's rein.

"That's enough, Melissa!" said Carie. "Mind your manners. If you aren't cold, you can just go down to the end of the canyon and put the poles up so's the horses don't wander off. After I eat and warm up, we'll be on our way."

The little girl, ashamed now of her outburst, quickly trotted away to do as she was told. Carie smiled at the small departing back. "Please forgive her, Ranger. Will tells everybody that she'd be a pretty good kid if she weren't so much like me."

"Ma'am, amazing little granddaughter you have there," John chuckled. "No need for forgiveness, for the little spitfire has given me the first fun I've had in years!"

Faces now somber, their eyes met in complete understanding. Later, as John finished rubbing down the mule, Missy came darting past him. She sat crosslegged near Carie who was resting beside the fire, stroking Boots' head in her lap. "Tell me about Bird Man," Carie said softly.

Missy, for once, could not utter a sound, so John covered for the little girl and related the events of Bird Man's death.

"Thank you for burying him, Ranger, for he deserved only the best. He was our first friend when we set up the sawmill for the fort. He was good to both man and beast; he taught us the ways of nature, the land and animals, and he believed as we did, that the Indian and the white man could live in harmony."

Shaking her head, Carie rose to her feet. "Those days have ended with Bird Man's passing."

"Why?" asked Missy, startled by her grandmother's words.

"To the Apache he was a holy man, and while he lived he kept the tribes from the war path. But now, not even a McKittrick will ever again be welcome in these mountains."

Seeing the child's stricken face, Carrie patted her.

"Don't worry, dear, they'll let us leave when they see the gifts we leave behind." Her voice was now strong with authority. "Please pour out the grain for the horses, John. Missy and I will see to those gifts. Oh, and I will need your rope."

"Sure thing, ma'am," the Ranger replied. Grasping the heavy rawhide baskets, he left the cave to pour the corn out in long lines for the horses.

Carie untied the reata from John's saddle and, using a Bowie knife, quickly cut the rope into four pieces. "Stuff your pockets full with corn, Missy. We'll catch four of the paint mares while the Ranger is pouring out the feed."

Understanding now what her grandmother planned to leave as gifts, she did as she was told, asking only, "Which ones, Gran Carie?"

"You catch that big black-and-white pin-eared mare, and the one with the glass eyes that you kids called Crystal. I'll get old Soapy and Pretty One."

"Do we have to give up Pretty One?" Missy gasped.

Carie couldn't force herself to look into the child's stricken face as she deftly fashioned four halters from the pieces of rope.

"I know it's hard, Missy, but we must leave a special horse for Chief Espejo, and Pretty One is as good as they come."

Missy, drying her eyes on her sleeve, could only nod in agreement.

"All right then, let's go," Carie said.

The Ranger watched with interest as the two women moved among the herd. Catching the mares seemed to present no problem for them.

John had no way of knowing that the care of all of the McKittrick colts was the responsibility of Meri, Missy, and Willie. On being weaned, at six to seven months old, the colts were taken to the ranch headquarters where they received months of loving, gentle handling by the youngsters, who spent hours each day working with each colt, all under the close tutelage of Carie and the watchful eye of old Feliz.

One by one, Carie and Feliz would rope a colt and yoke it to one of the big mules, and the children took turns leading the mule 'round and 'round the corral, tugging the young horse until it no longer resisted and followed wherever led. Next, the children would stake the colts to large wagon wheels that had been laid on the ground. The colts learned not only to stand tied hour after hour, day after day, but they gained confidence that their young masters would hand-feed them and water them. They nickered a welcome when they heard the children's soft whistles as they approached, struggling with the heavy pails of grain or water.

The conditioning that followed was pure pleasure for the little horses. Each was brushed daily from head to tail, and it was hilarious to watch as they wriggled and stretched as the children scratched their withers and backs. The colts soon learned to nip playfully and shove one another to be first groomed.

In their last months at the ranch, the colts' schooling became serious as they learned the feel of being strapped with a surcingle and became tolerant of the weight of the saddle. Mishaps occurred daily. Once Willie was dragged the entire length of the corral by an errant mule colt as he attempted to harness the long-eared beast.

Meri suffered rope-burned hands when she struggled to hold a black filly as it bucked across the barnyard in a vain attempt to eject the hated saddle from its back. Missy laughed and jeered at her siblings, but it ceased to be funny when she herself was bitten on the arm by an irascible paint who thought he wasn't being given enough feed. All was taken in stride as Lea ministered to a bloody nose, rope burns, and not only a bruised body but the ego of a mighty enraged little girl. Carie, meanwhile, worked in the barn late into the night applying salve to the equally banged-up animals.

Upon reaching two years old, the fillies were separated from the horse colts and sent back to the herd. They were far too valuable as brood mares, so few were ever ridden. Their brothers were sent to a secluded camp near Wild Rose Pass to be broken and trained to the saddle. Only the mule colts were sold to farmers who held the rich, fertile lands of Redford and Presidio on the Rio Grande and were eager buyers.

The daily chores, through rain or shine, winter's bitter north winds or the blistering heat of the intense summer sun, never seemed like work to the McKittricks. Each year brought the blessing of a new crop of colts, due to the breeding program begun years before by Will and carried on by Carie. She bred Skye's Son to the best of the mares and borrowed the services of a mountain-raised Spanish stud from her neighbor, George Jones, for Skye's Son's daughters. This produced tough, sure-footed grulla and dun colts. A big red jackass was borrowed from a Mexican farmer, Señor Hidalgo, and this completed the program.

Hero was bred to twenty of the tallest and largest

boned of the mares, and his get was a boon to the family's coffers. In return and as payment Carie allowed each of the two men to select five of his animal's offspring. This not only improved the McKittrick herd but also benefitted their good friends and neighbors.

Now, as Carie moved through the herd selecting the four designated mares, her little shadow, Missy held out hands full of golden grain, and Carie easily slipped the makeshift halters over the mares' heads. With each of their colts following, Carie led them to the oak grove near the pond, tying each securely. Missy continued to feed the mares until the last kernel was gone from her pockets, lingering only near Pretty One's side to pat and rub the head of the beautiful red-and-white paint mare.

"You be a good girl, Pretty One, and they'll treat you nice."

"Time to leave, Missy," came the quiet voice by her side. "I want you to take the lead, so catch Alice for yourself and I'll get Mona for the Ranger. They're both saddle broke, and ol' Hammer's good enough for me. We'll turn Skye's Son loose and he can help keep the strays in line."

Not a word was spoken as the mounts were saddled and the remaining supplies from the cave were packed into saddle bags. As they mounted, Carie nodded to Missy and, at the signal, the little girl let out a piercing whistle. The horses pricked up their ears and began to follow their leader down the canyon.

John and Carie stayed back with the tethered "gift" mares until the last of the herd disappeared beyond the trees. Carie then turned to the Ranger. "Lope on ahead and help Missy. I'll ride drag." The man complied, lightly touching his spurs to his horse's sides. He caught up with the herd as they were turning north out of the canyon toward their destination, and he looked back to where he had left Carie.

The scene he beheld was so chilling that he pulled cruelly on his horse's mouth to abruptly rein her to a stop.

Carie had ridden out into a clearing beyond the trees and was waving in salute to more than a hundred mounted Indian braves lined out on the high ridge above, their horses standing still as stone. The icy wind ruffled the feathers of their headdress and the manes of the animals. The silence was deafening, with only the whisper of the wind sighing among the pines.

"Espejo! *Vaya con Dios!*" shouted Carie.

The tribesmen raised their feather-trimmed spears in salute and let forth a resounding whoop to honor Carie McKittrick. The roaring echo bounced off the walls of the canyon, and the herd of horses and mules panicked into a stampede. Mona reared and almost jumped out from under the Ranger, and he had his hands full in not only trying to control the mare but to stay on as she darted over rocks and around brush in pursuit of the herd.

Missy was suddenly at his side, her little gray under control. "Let 'em run," she yelled, "they'll tire after a mile or so! Just keep 'em headed north!"

Missy sped away as quickly as she had appeared, leaving the Ranger shaking his head in wonder as to which way was north. As he tried to get his bearings, he concentrated on controlling the unruly Mona and began to notice that the horses were no longer running in fear but for the pure joy of the run. Bred for centuries to run with manes and tails flying, the strong Thoroughbreds raced one another across the high mountain mesa until, one by one, they began to slow. Nickers were heard from mare and colt alike as they stopped to pair up. Mona finally responded to John's guidance and pranced daintily, nickering with the rest. Only then did John Revell realize that he was shaking uncontrollably.

"Wasn't that fun?" came the cheery voice of the little girl as she rode up.

"Fun! Why, you little idiot! We came close to being scalped on the one hand, and run down on the other!"

Missy's face, flushed by the abrasive cold wind, glowed with pleasure as she reported, "Espejo and his tribe were just thanking Gran Carie for the gifts, Johnny Reb. And as for the horses, they just needed a little spark to have some fun!"

"Har-rumph!" came the reply, but the Ranger couldn't help smiling back at the sparkling eyes of the happy little girl.

"We'd best get moving, 'cause there comes Gran Carie, and she won't like us to be a-dallyin'," the child said seriously. Whistling to the herd, Missy loped the gray Alice forward to lead the herd. A feeling of warmth and comfort stole over the man's body and he, too, whistled. His mount, Mona, in disgust at his puny effort, backed her ears and snorted in reply.

/\.\/\.\/\

Some forty-five miles to the south, Will and Billy Frank huddled at the back of the cave. It was in no way similar to Bird Man's cave, aside from the fact that it was gouged from the huge outcropping of rock created eons ago by molten lava.

On the bend of a dry creekbed, this cave was formed over time by the force of rushing water resulting from fierce seasonal rainstorms. Gradually, as the heavy rainfall drained downward from the mountains into each canyon draw, it would eventually flow into Little Warrior Creek, deepening not only its bed, but rushing around the bend to form the cave. Year after year, inch by inch, the cave had become a mammoth opening some fifty feet wide and more than a hundred feet deep.

Because of the cave's advantageous location some forty miles from the Rio Grande it had been used for refuge for centuries, first by wandering Aztecs and later by Spaniards traveling to and from Mexico. But it was from the bandits it received its infamous name, Rustler's Cave. Cortina and other marauders of that ilk routinely used it as a strategic place to hole up after burning, stealing, and pillaging the gringo settlements north of the border. Here they would rest and feed and water their animals. The surrounding land, being somewhat flat, was covered with protein-rich blue and black grama grass, side-oats grama, curly mesquite, and weeds of every description. This high country provided not only food for the range animals but also breathtaking beauty for the human eye.

The mesa country also held an abundance of mule deer and antelope, game that was savored by all men— brown, white, and golden-skinned. Had it not been for the pesky coyote, the sly bobcat, the hated mountain lion, and an occasional brown bear, this country could have been called paradise. Those "varmints" were tolerated, however, because their pelts felt mighty good in the wintertime. Their strength and power also commanded healthy respect, because each could destroy or maim its target in the blink of an eye.

It was to this picturesque place that Will and Billy Frank had been brought, five days before, by Chango Gomez and his thirty-member gang.

Will cursed as he thought how easily he and Billy Frank had ridden into the bandit trap. The fall day could not have been more perfect. The sun, balanced against the clear blue sky lightly sprinkled with fluffy clouds, cast moving shadows across the mesa, its warmth bringing a feeling of wellbeing to the wranglers' tired bodies. Both Will and Billy Frank had been at point in front of the cattle when the ambushers rose out of the tall grass on two sides of the herd and cut down all six of the McKittricks' cowboys. Will and Billy Frank were surrounded and captured without having fired a shot.

"What's the matter, Papa, your hand hurting?" whispered Billy Frank.

"No, son." Will smiled at the slim, bearded man at his side. "just disgusted with myself for being so careless."

"You were no more at fault than me, Papa. Thought we were far enough from the border to not expect trouble."

"No excuse to lose six good men." Will winced as he spat out the words.

Concern crossed the face of the younger man. "You sure you're all right? Damn, I wish I could do something to ease your pain."

Will, trying to hide the anguish he felt, held up the

poorly bandaged hand. "It doesn't throb as much now and, due to that Chinese cook's branding the wound, there doesn't seem to be any infection. It's the cold and dampness that's working on this old body. How are you doing?"

"I'm fine, Papa," Billy Frank answered. Shivering, he pulled a thin blanket across his body. "But the chill of this cave is getting to my jakeleg, too."

For all Will McKittrick's physical prowess and strength, he had an unabashed tenderness when it came to this beloved son, so he quickly turned his head away as shame brought tears to his eyes. "I'm sorry, son, you have suffered more than your due with the loss of your leg at Gettysburg. Now, I've got us in a worse mess, leading us into a trap like a damned greenhorn."

Billy Frank clasped the older man's shoulder and smiled again into Will's face. "You know, what's really bothering me most is the smell of so many unwashed bodies and the rancid smell of whatever it is that your Chinaman is cooking. Hope we're not getting your finger for dessert."

Will couldn't help laughing aloud, which instantly brought a small, wiry Mexican to their side.

"Ah, Señor Will, again I must warn you not to disturb our game of cards!" Gomez chided, twisting his greasy moustache. "There is nothing you need to talk about. Just think of the little gray one who will soon bring the *caballos*. Which reminds me, Manuel came in from Carrasco a short time ago. He says the señora has agreed to take fifty to my *estancia*, this is good, no? At most, I expected only thirty, so she must persuade your neighbors to give her the extra. Which means you have a few more days to *think*—ten days Carrasco gave the señora. Nice of him, *verdad?*" Gomez sneered through tobacco-stained teeth and laughed. "But it was I who was the smart one, to send to her your finger!" The sardonic smile left the evil face and he spat his chaw directly onto Will's boot. "Just pray to your *Dios* that she gets here soon," he growled, "for I am thinking of sending your *whole hand* to her next time, instead of just a finger!" Laughing with maniacal derision, Gomez turned and strutted back to his card game.

Like a banty rooster, thought Will.

"Acts like he's the smartest rooster in the barnyard, don't he, Pa?"

"Just what I was thinkin', Billy Frank. And, speaking of thinking, that's just about all I've done since we got here. Knowing your mother like I do, I never had any doubt as to what she will do, but there is sure as hell one thing I know she *won't* do and that's to let this sorry bunch have our horses. She spent the four years we were gone hiding them, from first one army, then another, and running from this kind of riffraff!"

"And what is it you are so sure she *will* do, Papa?"

"Why, she'll come and get us, son."

"You got that right!" Billy Frank chuckled and pulled the blanket up to his mouth to stifle the sound.

Concerned, Will shook his head. "In the meantime, Son, let's keep quiet—like the sawed-off runt told us—and think. Let's study each one of this bunch and see what we're up against."

The fleeting mirth drained from the younger man's eyes as he surveyed the group clustered around the fire in the center of the cave. "Been doin' that, Pa, and I think that in all my years in the service I have never seen a worse bunch. Those two off by themselves at the entrance—I figure they must have been deserters from the rebs. How do you figure they got hooked up with this outfit?"

Will only shook his head. He studied the hard faces of the huddled pair, obviously Anglo, their dirty blond hair hanging in greasy strings beneath their hats. "Notice how much alike they are? Must be kin, maybe even brothers. And there's three more Anglos with that group playing cards at the left of the fire."

Billy Frank swore under his breath, "Yeah, Pa, that big one that's as hairy as a gorilla. He's the one that held you down when Gomez cut off your finger. Those two Mexicans next to him held your legs."

Will set his jaw and gritted his teeth to control his rising rage. "They were just following orders. Gomez is the one I have to settle the score with."

"That's the one thing I don't understand, Pa. How does that little devil control this bunch? Any one of them could flatten him in a minute."

"His gun, Billy Frank," Will answered with contempt. "Like the small, mountain rattler that's just as deadly as a six-foot diamondback. He controls them with the fastest gun I've ever seen in my life, so, in the long run, they *fear* him. Their fear is his power."

"You may be right, Pa, but there's three men here that don't fear him."

The older man's eyes, questioning, locked into those of his son. "Three?"

"Yes, Pa. For one, that Chinese cook. You notice he never says a word, just grunts when Gomez issues orders. But his eyes never leave that little general when he's not looking, and they read only hate."

Will nodded. "And the other two?"

"Why, that's you and me, Pa."

3

Meri

THE CREEK WATER felt good to Meri as Stretch and the six geldings splashed in the shallows. Each icy droplet hitting her face helped ease the rapid beating of her heart caused by the frenzy of leaving.

"Might feel good now, fellas," she said, speaking softly to the horses, "but hold 'er down a bit. We've got five miles to go in this creek, and with a norther comin' in, I don't think I want to get a chill from getting a bath from you!"

As she reached the first bend in the creek, Meri pulled Stretch to a stop and turned in her saddle to look back at Feliz standing on the far bank, watching her depart. The old Mexican swung his rawhide reata in a circle above his head.

"*Vaya con Dios, chiquita mia,*" he shouted.

Meri raised her hand in answer and tried to speak, but raw emotion rose in her throat and she was unable to respond. For the first time she realized how completely alone and truly frightened she was, and her legs began to tremble so violently that her boots made a tapping noise in the stirrups. Her horse, sensing her stress, snorted and shook his head. This had the calming effect the girl needed. Gritting her teeth, she turned back in the saddle and said, "I'm okay, boy. Let's go!" The tall bay Thoroughbred instantly responded and began to take short, quick steps through the water and over the moss-covered rocks.

The geldings, rested and frisky, followed for the first mile, bunching up behind her, irritating both Meri and her mount. They playfully nipped at each other, each trying to gain a position at her side. Stretch finally grew tired of their antics and reached out to nip at those closest to his side. The unruly bunch shied away and tried to go to the bank to get out of the stream. Meri yelled angrily as she jerked on the long lead ropes.

"Stop that, dern you! Get back in line! Come on, fellas, settle down!"

The sound of their mistress' voice told them she would tolerate no more foolishness. The horses quickly turned back into the stream. After a half hour of plodding in the creek, they placidly dropped back into a single file behind the bay.

The shallow stream angled to the southeast, away from the McKittrick spread and the fort town, and there it disappeared underground. In normal conditions, after a couple of miles it would reappear from under the rocks and pebbles to meet with the stronger, spring-fed

Limpia. The left fork turned northeast through Limpia Canyon, while the right fork came gurgling out and continued its flow some hundred miles to the south. Time and again it mysteriously disappeared and reappeared on its journey to the Great River, the Rio Grande. However, on this late October day, the abundant fall rains had filled the deep underground cisterns and water gushed upward to the surface.

Similar to the dry creek where her father and grandfather were being held, these banks had been eroded by time and the elements, creating a miniature canyon that made a perfect concealed passage for Meri and her geldings. That is, if no one happened to be drinking from, fishing from, or simply crossing the creek.

Gran Carie has planned well, thought the girl. With the temperature dropping and a large noon meal under their belts, most of the people at the fort will stay inside and take a long siesta.

This gave Meri a feeling of security, and she was reassured by the thought of the strong geldings she led. The horses were in good shape from their daily portions of precious grain and prairie hay and also from being ridden every day by the McKittrick children.

Stretch, the Thoroughbred Meri rode, was a lean, sixteen-hand, nine-year-old bay. He was used (as Carie often boasted) "to go a long way in a hurry." And, just for fun, Meri had raced him against all comers on fiesta days at the fort. No ranch in the area had raised a faster horse than Stretch.

The gelding, Operator, was the same age as Stretch. He actually did nothing well, yet he was much loved by Lea. The way she put it was, "Maybe I can't do anything fancy like the rest of you, but Operator has the easiest trot, is by far the most gentle, and his best features are those big, brown eyes. I love that horse!" Meri fondly recalled the time her mother had said that and, on hearing it, her dad, Billy Frank, grabbed his wife and swung her wildly around until they both toppled to the ground. "So, you love that dumb horse, do you!" he shouted into her grinning face. "Why, you can't even get his number, but you can sure get mine!" And so it was, that when any of us saw Lea with Operator, the McKittrick children smiled with love.

Bubbles, a youngster at six, was a red dun, just fifteen hands tall, but built like a locomotive. He was the pride and joy of young Willie. No one liked to ride the rotund little horse because he had such a round back and hardly any withers for a large saddle to sit on, much less fit right. Willie, however, discovered that his small saddle molded itself against the flat, fat back, and the horse's wonderful running-walk could keep up with any of the others at their fast trot. The way Willie put it, "He's solid comfort!"

Pelote was a grulla and, at twelve, was in his prime. His dam had been a Spanish-bred grulla mare that Will had bought from a neighboring rancher soon after he had moved into the area. Will needed a crossbreed that had already adapted to the rough terrain, and by breeding to his Thoroughbred stallion, had been rewarded with an animal as hardy and sure-footed as a mountain goat. Pelote not only carried the Spanish mare's sturdy qualities but also the mixed-bloodline traits—a blaze face, four stocking legs, and a flowing mane and tail. Carie always said Pelote was Will's favorite to show off when he went to town. All agreed, for it was a sight to see big Will McKittrick riding ramrod straight on the flashy animal.

Fargo, at ten, was a massive, bright sorrel, all seventeen hands of him. Before the war, when the McKittricks still had cattle, Billy Frank had roped and dragged calves, cows, and even bulls, day after day, on the big horse, and Fargo never tired. Every night as Billy Frank wearily pulled the saddle from Fargo's back, he'd think, *Fargo, you just don't know when to quit!*

Duke was too pretty to be true and was the love of Missy's life. At eight years, fine-boned and regal, the golden Palomino with white mane and tail was as handsome as a horse could be. Duke had been raised by Missy as a dogie, or motherless colt; his dam had been killed by a mountain lion. Missy had bottle-fed him from the time he was two months old, and all alone she trained him to bridle and saddle. She could ask anything of him and he would try to do it for her. It was a joy just to watch the sun-golden horse follow Missy around like a dog and stand patiently at the back door of the ranch house when she happened to be inside. Duke wasn't dumb, for he knew the little girl would always manage to raid the sugar bowl for him.

Last but not least of the horses in Meri's care, Pretty Boy caused a bewildered look on many a stranger's face when they visited the McKittricks. Pretty Boy had to be the ugliest paint horse ever to draw breath—and also just about the meanest! No one knew how old he was or where he'd come from—he just turned up one day. Feliz found him standing at the barn door, poor as a snake, and matted all over with long white, black and gray hair. Feliz fattened him up, and each day the girls had taken turns brushing his thick coat, but to no avail. He still looked more like a large Spanish goat than a horse. But to kind, gentle Meri, he was a prince. Even though any rider could shoot a gun while mounted on a McKittrick horse, seldom would any horse allow a freshly-killed deer or beef or anything that smelled of blood to be packed on his back. It was Meri who found that Pretty Boy would allow it. And he packed many an animal in from the high country, saving a lot of time and riding, because no one had to go for a wagon. His major problem, however, was not his looks. Pretty Boy was a kicker! No one except Meri or Carie dared get near his rear. Even Will warned, "Don't go near his hind legs! That damned horse won't kick Meri because she's blind to his sorry looks. Nor Carie, because no horse would dare kick her." With that accurate statement, the dark Irishman would roar with laughter.

It would be quite a sight, therefore, had anyone come upon Meri as she led the six geldings down the stream. Where Missy molded herself to become one with her horse, Meri was poetry in motion. Her tall and graceful body flowed with the movement of the handsome bay. The banks of the creek were steep and lined with cottonwood and creek willow, now painted yellow by an early frost. It was quiet, with only the sound of splashing water and hoofs striking the rocks. Trying to distract herself from the terror being suffered by her father and grandfather, Meri amused herself by watching for fish, frogs, or turtles that might flop from the water or creekbank. So intently was she gazing at the creek that she was unaware of being watched from above. Her attention was caught by the sight of a large catfish, so quietly still near the grassy bank that only the slightest movement of his gills indicated he was still alive.

The rope sailed out from over the top of the bluff and settled around her waist and arms, burning as it tightened. She was brutally yanked from Stretch's back as the big bay lunged forward in fright, and she hit the bank so hard that it knocked the breath from her lungs. The geldings bolted into one another in the center of the stream, and Pretty Boy lost his footing on the slimy, moss-covered rocks, falling hard on his side. His lead rope tightened and jerked the other horses to a stop, but he soon regained his footing, rearing up from the water. All stood still, eyes wide, with their heads and ears turned toward the bluff.

A man appeared, tugging cruelly on the rope that gripped Meri. His dark face was covered in a thick, coarse beard, and stringy black hair stuck out from under a filthy black hat. Beady eyes glistened as he sucked in breath at the sight of the lovely girl lying captive on the bank.

"Well, well, Señorita, what do we have here?" laughed a harsh, Spanish voice. "Carrasco say you would be bringing horses to us, but not so soon, eh?"

Meri struggled to force air past the tightness in her chest, but she could neither speak nor move.

"You not hurt, pretty one?" The Mexican calmly moved down the bluff, coiling the rope to keep it taut as he approached. He stood over the wounded girl, leering, "No, you not hurt, but you will be hurting with great love for Gregorio when I'm through with you!" With a fiendish laugh, he bent over to loosen her bonds. "Carrasco, he say we can keep any womans we find with the horses. What a great surprise, when this gran hombre brings you in!"

Meri fought rising panic and closed her eyes briefly to hide her fear and regain her composure. But seconds later, she jerked her head up, glared at him and blurted, "Gregorio Martinez, you're a damned fool if you think you can touch me! Now, let go of the rope and I'll forget this ever happened."

She struggled to get to her feet, but the Mexican's right foot caught her leg, causing her to fall again. Meri choked back a scream as he slammed her over onto her stomach and began to tie her hands behind her back.

Sensing the danger, the horses became restive as they watched Gregorio cruelly manhandling Meri. She clenched her teeth in pain to keep from crying out as the rope tightened around her wrists. As he rolled her over onto her back, she glared up at him and painfully spat, "I'll get you for this, Gregorio! But what will be worse—when I don't show up, Gran Carie will find you, and your life won't be worth a peso!" The Mexican just chuckled, and reached to slide a greasy hand across her chest.

"Ah, lovely señorita, I don't worry about the señora. Carrasco has plans for her." Seeing that Meri was securely bound, Gregorio rose and entered the stream to catch the spellbound horses. Pretty Boy, being at the end of the line, was closest, so the Mexican stomped through the water to him. As he approached the paint, the horse backed his ears and slowly turned away from the man. When Gregorio got to within three feet of the horse, the gelding let loose. One hind foot caught the man in the chin, and the other landed squarely on his chest. The young Mexican was dead before he hit the water.

A shocked Meri watched with mixed feelings of relief and nausea, but began to cry when she saw the blood from Gregorio's limp form drift in rivulets downstream. The distraught girl struggled with her bound hands and wondered aloud, "Now what on earth am I going to do?"

At the sound of her voice, the horses started moving toward the bank, stepping out of the water and onto the grassy bank, where they nipped at the green shoots. Pretty Boy, however, walked up to Meri and leaned his head down to smell her. Looking up at the ugly, ring-eyed paint, she couldn't help but smile. "Thanks for saving me, Pretty Boy, but I sure wish you knew how to untie these knots."

At that moment a perch flopped in the water, bringing Meri's attention back to the floating dead man staring grotesquely at nothing. "That's how I can get loose!" She painfully rolled herself back into the stream and, on her back, using her head and her bound feet, inched herself toward the dead man. She edged her shivering body over the rocky creekbed, sharp edges cutting into her already bruised arms, hands and wrists. The icy water rapidly filled the back of her brush jacket, running down her leggings and into her boots. Her head felt as though it might burst. A flow of adrenalin made her almost oblivious to the cold water, which actually prevented her from losing consciousness. Her body shivering and teeth chattering, Meri finally reached the corpse. Fighting a wave of nausea, she rolled over onto her knees and with her teeth drew the Mexican's eight-inch skinning knife from its sheath on his belt. The torturous journey back to the bank was worsened by water splashing into her mouth as she gripped the knife in her teeth. Choking, sometimes nearly strangled, she was determined not to drop the blade. After what seemed an eternity, she neared the bank and, without moving her body out of the water, dropped the knife onto the grassy bank. Exhausted now, she coughed, gasped, and filled her lungs with life-saving air. After a brief rest, she again took the knife in her teeth and buried it hilt first in the soft mudbank. Rolling over, she backed up to the exposed blade and, sitting up with her bound wrists against it, rubbed the rope against its razor-sharp edge until she was freed.

Rejoicing at release from the offending bonds, she became aware of the pain in her arms and shoulders. Meri worked her fingers to restore circulation so that she could grab the grassy turf and pull herself out of the water. Once there, she gave in to both the physical and mental pain, collapsing and sobbing into the sweet-smelling earth.

Pretty Boy didn't let her cry for long. He walked to her side, put his head down and blew his nose directly into her mud-covered face. The sobbing stopped and Meri, with a crooked smile, sat up saying, "Okay, I get the message, Pretty Boy. You saved me again!"

She crawled back into the water and quickly rinsed the grime from her face, hair, and clothes which were already wet and muddy. Back on dry land, she drew the knife from the mudbank, wiped it and slipped it into her belt. Then she moved stiffly to pick up Stretch's reins and the rope that tied the geldings one to the other.

"We're ready to go, boys!" She pulled herself up to mount the bay. "But this time, not in the creek. We've been found out—or will be when they find Gregorio's body—so we're takin' to solid ground." The geldings needed no urging. As she touched her spurs to Stretch's side, the horses all lunged up the face of the bluff and through the trees. Once again on flat land, Meri clucked them into a lope.

The rigorous activity of riding helped to warm her, but the cold wind blasted against her already chapped face and chilled body. She knew that she would soon have to stop to get out of her wet clothes or find some sort of shelter. She mulled over every mile of ground she was to cover and smiled as she remembered an old line shack near the place where the little creek turned to meet Limpia Canyon. Her spirits rose, and she urged her horse to go even faster. The geldings matched the pace with no restraint, and Meri soon caught sight of her destination.

As she expected, the one-room mud-and-straw house appeared to be deserted, but she cautiously reined the horses to a walk, riding slowly to its door, dismounted, and tied the lead rope to the horn of her saddle. She stood shivering as she looped Stretch's reins to the hitching post. Leaning into the door with her shoulder, she pushed it open and hastily looked around the room. Once fully inside, her heart sank and she thought aloud, "Oh my gosh, there's not one thing here I can use." She noted the rickety table, two broken chairs, and an empty cupboard. Then, with a yelp of joy, she spotted a small heap of fabric in one darkened corner. She stumbled across the room, grabbed at the dusty bundle and found it was a tarp, somewhat the worse for wear, but dry. "No wonder I missed it when I first came in; it looks like part of the dirt floor." Unmindful of the filth—and her sore hands—she took the tarp and laid it on the table. Grimacing, she drew Gregorio's knife from her belt and removed her wet jacket and leggings. She cut a hole in the center of the tarp and, bending over, slipped her head through the hole. As she straightened up, the tarp fell almost to the floor, resulting in a good wind-breaking poncho. When it was belted, she felt immediately warmer. Without further delay, she pulled open the door and, with more ginger in her step, moved quickly to Stretch's side. Her sudden movement startled the horse and he jumped back, almost breaking the reins.

"Whoa, Stretch," she said softly, "I'm sorry. It's only me," and she held a corner of the tarp for Stretch to smell. Comically, he blew his nose in disgust at the dirt, but he settled down to chew contentedly on his bits and remained calm while she tied the wet clothing to the back of her saddle. As her sore hands clumsily worked at the leather strings, she again thought how lucky it was that she had thought to keep the knife and that she had these wonderful animals to help her. Carefully she climbed onto the bay, smoothing the tarp snugly around her body. She called to her friends, "Well, boys, something tells me that if we can make the next six miles to Wild Rose Pass within two hours, we'll be in High Cloud's camp by nightfall!"

This time, as her strong horses kept a fast, bone-jarring trot at the girl's urging, Meri continuously scanned the countryside for any sign of human life. The tarp proved to be a blessing. Hanging halfway to the ground, it warmed her body and gradually began to dry her clothes. Except for her wet boots and her battered hands and wrists, she began to enjoy the beauty of the canyon and its wildlife.

The sun's fingers played a gentle melody of light and shadow on the rose-and-rust rock of Limpia's walls as the creek snaked its way northward; the canyon walls protected Meri from the sharp north wind. She kept to a centuries-old wildlife trail that meandered alongside to the creek, the ground soft with silt brought by the early fall rains. There were mule deer with the bucks' antlers already in velvet; there were 'coons, skunk, and porcupine. Coveys of quail rose from the brush and tall grass as she approached. As the waning daylight faded, doves flew in for a drink at the pools dotted along the canyon floor. All was quiet, and the girl was conscious only of the steady beat of the horses' hooves, with an occasional call of a white-winged dove, or the angry scream of a hawk to a golden eagle flying too near its nest, high in the lava rocks above.

As she neared the last steep climb to Wild Rose Pass, her stomach rumbled at the thought of a hot meal. It was still a half mile of easy slope to the top, so she urged Stretch and the geldings to maintain the long-held trot. She stood up in her stirrups to adjust the weight of her body to that of the horse. The others scrambled behind her, matching their pace to that of the bay, and they soon came to the bowl-shaped saddle of the pass.

Meri pulled Stretch to a stop. The horses' sides heaved from exertion, and one by one they blew their noses as if in relief. Meri looked at each one and, talking to herself, said aloud, "Guys, Gran Carie would want me to check your feet, but I don't know for the life of me how I'm going to get down." But she painfully started her descent from the bay. As she touched ground the pain in her knees struck with a vengeance, and she had to cling to the stirrup to keep from falling. As she laid her head against the horse's side, Stretch's nose touched her red cheek as if in sympathy. Meri jerked up in surprise and said, "Thanks again, old friend." She moved stiffly as she examined each of the horses' hooves before she continued the even steeper descent to the wide canyon below. With careful attention to each horse, she found all were in good shape, with the exception of Pretty Boy, who had a deep cut on his right forefoot. Probably from his fall in the creek, she thought. Speaking softly to the paint, Meri said, "I'm sorry, dear savior. I should have noticed this sooner. I'll just take off your halter, and you can follow us the rest of the way at your own pace." She gently slipped the grass halter from his head and rubbed him between his short, stubby ears. Pretty Boy, grateful at being released from his bonds, rubbed his head against her chest. Sighing, Meri looked across the two-mile-wide canyon below, then up at the 500-foot rock wall and bluffs on the mountain beyond. "Not far to High Cloud's camp now! Won't food and a warm fire make us feel good!"

Even though the activity had helped the girl's aching body, she still had difficulty mounting Stretch. The horse sensed her discomfort and stood stock still. As they started to move, the geldings knew they were near home and shelter, and they eagerly lunged forward, tucking their hind legs beneath them and sliding most of the way down to the bottom. When they reached the flat land, in unison they stationed themselves by the side of Stretch, and lengthened their strides into a long lope toward a thin trail of smoke spiraling lazily upward to meet the low-hanging clouds.

The young Indian had seen the rider and horses almost as soon as they had come over the horizon of the distant skyline. Ever on the alert for strangers, High Cloud held his rifle at ready upon seeing the fast-approaching horses and the rider cloaked in a strange fabric. As they neared to about a mile away, he recognized the McKittrick horses, and at one-half mile, his sharp eyes told him it was Meri. His bronzed face lit with joy, and he shouted, "Mer-ri-ii!" It was Meri, his blood sister, his playmate, his love!

By tribal ritual at age twelve, High Cloud had been made blood brother to the entire McKittrick family. White Cloud, his wise grandfather, had asked Will McKittrick to take the young brave and raise him to manhood. White Cloud knew that the Indians' days of freedom were numbered. The great chief had searched Will's black eyes and said, "I am getting old, and near the end of life's journey. My camp consists of only a small number of old women and braves. High Cloud is the last of our young, and the last of my bloodline. He should not be confined on a reservation, but should run free with the horses."

Neither Will nor Carie ever regretted their decision to take High Cloud. Over the years, he had proved to be a master at breaking young horses. He was gentle and kind, feeding them out of his hand and each day rubbing them with soft doeskin, weeks before he attempted to ride them. Then, when he felt they were ready, it was a sight to see. He would put a colt in the pen by itself, gently placing a grass halter with only one rein over its head. He would then open the gate, vault onto the horse's bare back, and allow the animal to run free. The strange and magical thing was that the horse would never buck, nor did High Cloud ever fall off; they just ran together as one.

Meri responded in a cracked voice breaking against the cold wind, "High Cloud!" she yelled, pushing Stretch even faster toward the welcome arms. She fought to conceal the emotion when she first saw her childhood companion running to close the distance between them. But as she slowed to a stop before him, she could neither move from her horse nor contain the flow of tears.

"Meri! What has happened?" he exclaimed as he put down his gun and stared in alarm at her bruised and tear-streaked face. He got no response. Meri simply leaned from the saddle and slid limply into his strong, muscled arms. In one fluid motion, High Cloud grasped her legs and, holding her body close to his, carried her quickly to his dugout. Never breaking his stride, he butted the door open with his shoulder, placed his precious burden near to the fire, and gently pulled the tarp from the whimpering girl.

"You must get out of these clothes, little one." But as Meri tried to untie the bands of her shirt, her fingers refused to respond; she could only look into High Cloud's concerned eyes and reach to softly touch his face with her stiff, cold fingers. High Cloud gently pulled away her hands. "Meri, let me undress you. We must get these wet clothes off before you become sick." His voice cracked with emotion, "I will be careful." She could only nod in assent. Slowly, and with the care normally taken with a baby, he gently removed her clothes and soggy boots. Apparently oblivious to her shapely body, he quickly grabbed a rug lying before the fire and wrapped it around her trembling body. He again pulled her into his arms, rocking her as one would rock a child. Only when he felt the warmth of his body had eased her chill did he give in to his building anger.

"Meri, do you think you can tell me about it now? Who did this to you? Please! Tell me, so I will know what I must do!" With her last remaining energy the young girl nodded, and haltingly began.

"It all started this morning when Gran Carie came home from the fort. . . ." As she unfolded the tale, his compassionate expression never changed, but he was choking back his inner rage. Only when she came to the abrupt end of her story, sobbing uncontrollably, did he move. With trembling hand he brushed the tears from her battered face.

"You are with me now, Meri, and I will take care of you," he said quietly, as her sobs began to subside. "I will get a tub of water for you to warm yourself and bathe. While you are doing that I will tend the horses."

A frown crossed the girl's face, and the tears were replaced by concern. "Oh, High Cloud, how selfish of me! They have been so good all day, and I know they must be so tired."

The boy's heart jumped as he beheld with joy the change in his beloved sister. He chuckled as she added, "And please look for Pretty Boy. I let him loose up on the pass. when I stopped to check the geldings' feet. He has a bad cut on his right forefoot!"

High Cloud carefully laid Meri on the floor and moved quickly to get a kettle of hot water from the fireplace, pouring it into a large wooden tub. He brought buckets of water from the trough that led from the outside through the wall of the dugout to the inside, and he continued until the tub was almost full. Only when he was satisfied that the temperature was right did he speak.

"There is soap and a blanket to dry yourself, little one, and you will find clothes in the trunk by the bed." His voice became harsh. "You must get up, Meri, and clean yourself. I will not have you get sick!"

"Oh, bosh, High Cloud, aren't you getting bossy!" The girl grinned at his departing back as he opened the door and slipped into the night.

High Cloud found Pretty Boy standing patiently just outside the door. He led the animal to a stall in the cedar-topped shed where he doctored the wound. Then he unsaddled Stretch and rubbed him down. After all the geldings were fed, watered, and secured for the night in the shed, he hastily returned to the dugout.

Meri was seated before the fire with the blanket wrapped tightly around her. As she turned her head toward him, he was almost blinded with rage, for the cleansing had uncovered the scratches and a large bruise on the right side of her face. As her arms reached out toward him, he could see the torn flesh on her wrists and hands. He cleared his throat before he spoke, to ensure that his voice would not betray his fury.

"I have taken care of your animals, and all are well." A fleeting smile crossed his face. "Even the brave Pretty Boy." His heart lifted as Meri's face transformed.

"Oh, thank you, High Cloud, I am so relieved!"

"The wind and sleet have been blowing hard from the north all afternoon, so I had already brought my brother Will's young horses to shelter in the corral next to the rock bluffs. If you are able, we can leave at first light for San Martine Springs to meet Gran Carie."

"Oh, no," replied Meri, "we don't need to get away until the day after tomorrow. Gran Carie had no idea your horses would already be here; she was sure we'd have to round them up. Also, she has the longest distance to go to meet Missy and help gather the mares and colts."

The young man smiled with relief. "That is good, for it will give you and Pretty Boy time to get your looks back!"

Meri laughed. "I'm the only one who can see what a beauty Pretty Boy really is!"

High Cloud chuckled. He was pleased to see color returning to Meri's face. "Well, then, we'll put some salve on your ugly face and hands, and afterward, I'm going to fill your unattractive body with food!" He skillfully dodged the shard of firewood that came sailing across the room.

Later, he again cradled the exhausted Meri before the fire and, brushing the wisps of tangled hair from her forehead, whispered in her ear, "Rest well, my dear little sister. We will not only help, we will free the men and bring them home. To the great Will and Gran Carie I owe my life for what they have done for me and for my people."

/\/\/\/\

As the cold north wind continued its relentless journey southward, one by one the lanterns of Fort Davis flickered on, and a rider came galloping in to stop in front of the trading post. He jumped down from his horse and, without taking time to tie the animal, rushed through the door.

"Carrasco!" he yelled, approaching the table where the outlaw sat drinking with four companions. "Carrasco! I have found Gregorio dead in the creek! *Dios mio!* I rode out to relieve him like you tol' me, and found him beaten like someone had hit him with a chain!"

Carrasco jumped from his chair and yelled out as he crossed the room to the door, "Come, compadres, pronto! I feel the Gran Carie has already made her move!"

The motley crew arrived at the creek and, with torches lighting their way, waded and splashed through to the corpse, its eyes still staring vacantly at the dark sky. Carrasco growled as he jerked the corpse from the water. "It was no chain, Vasquez, I can see from here the print of a hoof on his chin." Grasping the body with one hand, he tore open the dead man's bloody shirt. "Aye-ee! The other hoof burst Gregorio's heart!" The other men's eyes bugged out in fright, and they crossed themselves. Carrasco sneered and dropped the corpse back into its watery grave. "Drag him to the bank and leave him, Chacón, then ride to the house of his wife and tell her to come bury him. We will go back and get more men and supplies, for we must be at the McKittrick place by the first light of day to see what trick the Gran Señora is trying to pull!"

When the frightened onlookers didn't move, Carrasco lashed out with his huge fat hand, striking the nearest man so hard in the face that he fell across the corpse. The man screamed as if he had been as mortally wounded as the dead, but Carrasco only laughed and, with lips curled in a snarl, he said, "Pépe, you and Chacón go get that drunk gringo out of the shed behind the trading post and follow this creek to Limpia. Someone goes this way, I am sure." Turning to the wet man scrambling from the water he barked, "You, Manuel! Go to Gomez and tell him this time to cut off the hand from the big man, and maybe so have a little fun with his one-leg son!" Laughing cruelly as the group trudged back through the creek, he exhorted, "Come, amigos! Now we have our fun with the McKittrick women! Now we show that old bitch what great men we are!"

4

Lea and Willie

THE COLD WIND bit at the faces of Lea and Willie as Carie and her mule disappeared into the oak pine of the mountainside.

"Mama, I don't see her anymore. Shouldn't we go?"

Willie's comment brought Lea's thoughts back to the task to be done, and she lowered her hand to rest on her son's small shoulder. "Yes, we must go. . . ." Trying to conceal her apprehension from the boy, she groped for words to lighten the moment. "Hop up, Willie! Just think, we'll be down to Barrel Springs in a little while, and there our part in the scheme of things will come in." She reached tenderly to adjust Carie's jacket around his small frame and pulled Carie's hat almost down over his ears.

Willie squirmed and his face crinkled as he asked, "What's a 'skeen,' Mama?"

A fleeting smile crossed Lea's face as she replied, "Why, that's the plan of what we'll do to help get Papa and Grandpa Will back."

"Oh," Willie replied happily, as he watched his mother move to the front of the wagon and unwrap the lines from the wagon's brake. The lone mule, Hit, was hitched to the wagon, minus his partner. Lea patted the huge mule's forehead, saying, "Hit's a big part of the scheme, Willie. You'll see."

"Oh, Mama, let's go now!" blurted the impatient boy.

Lea was relieved to have hidden her nervousness, but she still had to struggle to make her tense body climb onto the wagon seat. Willie bounded up onto the seat and happily clapped his hands as his mama clucked to the mule, "Come on, Hit, we'll take it slow, fella, since you don't have old Hammer to help you." But the mule responded quickly to the gentle tug on the snaffle in his mouth, and he stepped out into the ruts in the road as though he still had Hammer by his side. Carie's horse, Chance, maintained a slow trot to keep pace.

The ride westward around the mountains to the slope leading to the H-O Canyon had always been considered a long but easy one. But when Carie had departed into the bowls of the sinister-looking mountains, the cold and sleet made its first real bite against the faces of mother and son. Lea's usually stoic expression creased in lines of worry as the sky rapidly turned dreary gray, and her spirits dropped proportionately as the daylight diminished.

It was not only for her beloved husband and her father-in-law that she feared but also for Carie and what she had to do. *Everything rides on that little woman's shoulders; the rest of us are just pawns,* she thought. *Carie's not a young woman anymore and to ride in this weather all night to reach Missy, why, I just don't know how she'll ever be able to make it.*

Just then a wagon wheel hit a large rock, causing the wagon to bounce and nearly overturn, and Hit lunged against the traces in fright. But as the wagon jolted upright, Willie yelled in admonition, "Mama! Watch where you're goin'!" Then he pointed joyously toward a stand of wind-burned willows swaying in the distance. "Barrel Springs! Our skeen of things!"

As Hit was reined to a stop under the delicate trees, Lea and Willie sat motionless in their seats, transfixed by the sight of the springs. More than five thousand gallons of water gushed from under the rocks, rushing into not one but several streams that flowed into a valley twenty to thirty miles wide and over forty miles long, providing life-giving water to man and beast alike.

"Mama," whispered Willie in awe, "ever' time we come here I can't help but wonder if it'll stop. How can that much water just keep on comin' out?"

Lea smiled down at the little face with the large hat comically almost over his eyes. "I feel the same way, Willie," she replied. "I guess everyone does. It's truly one of the good Lord's greatest blessings for this beautiful country." Pointing to the vast valley below, Lea continued, "Look, son! Antelope! Aren't they beautiful!"

But the boy had already grown rigid with excitement at seeing the graceful animals as they darted from sight.

"The north doesn't look good, Willie, and it's sure getting cold. Best we hurry and unhitch Hit and get Chance unsaddled." As Willie scrambled down to do his mother's bidding, she added, "Be sure and hobble them to graze, after you've let them drink their fill. I'll build a fire, and when you're finished, you can help me drape the tarp over the wagon for shelter from the wind. We'll sleep cozy underneath!"

.\.\/.\

Mother and son busily went about their tasks, unaware of the dark figure watching them from a small hill, concealed by the limbs of huge cedars. The man observed them for a time, then shrugged and moved deeper into the boughs of the strong-smelling trees. "Well, well," he whispered softly to himself, "what I took to be two women coming down the road turns out to be a woman and a lad. Don't know why they'd be way out here on a night like this, 'cept they be in trouble. Well, whatever's their problem, I'm not gettin' involved. I've got troubles enough of my own." He then pushed the branches aside and moved stealthily toward his horse tied in the draw on the far side of the hill. He mounted and rode eastward, never making his presence known to Lea and Willie.

The man didn't get far. About halfway to the fort, just four miles from the McKittrick ranch, cold and darkness took its toll. Finding another large cedar, he stopped, pulled the branches aside, and both man and horse took shelter for the night.

By morning, fog and sleet carpeted the valleys and bottomlands. That was why, at the entrance to the McKittrick spread, the stranger happened onto Carrasco and his men, who had also been delayed by the fog. The man had been startled by the sight of so many riders appearing suddenly over the white-blanketed hill. The *vaqueros* were typically dressed, from their large sombreros and the gleaming silver conchos on their colorful clothing to the large roweled spurs jingling with each step of their prancing steeds.

"*Buenos dias, señor,*" called out Carrasco pleasantly, reining his heavily laden horse to a stop squarely in front of the stranger. "My name is Carrasco de Monseis. I run the trading post at the fort. I see you have come from the west, and I wonder if you have met anyone on the road?"

"Glad to meet you. Name's Freeman." The man reached to grasp the fat hand extended by Carrasco. "I was trying to make the fort last night but had to stop because of the early dark." Hesitating, he continued, "As far as seeing anyone, I did see a woman and a boy at that big spring about ten miles back. Strangest thing, though, I thought it was two women when I first saw 'em. Didn't realize it was a boy until the lad stepped down from the wagon they was in, and his coat dang near drug the ground." He looked questioningly at Carrasco. "You lookin' for 'em?"

Carrasco's face lit up in a big, toothy smile. "Sí, señor, 'tis my silly wife. She got mad at me and ran off with our son. Thank you for your help and have a safe journey to the fort!"

The two parted, turning their backs to each other, Freeman continuing toward the fort and the other saying, "*Vamos, compadres,*" and the group of riders turned into the road leading to the McKittrick ranch house and corrals. Carrasco turned to the vaquero at his side, saying, "Tomás, go back to the top of the hill and kill that gringo! We want no word to get to anyone about what we are doing!"

A short time later, Carrasco and his men were ransacking the McKittrick house and barn. The sound of a single shot reverberated through the canyon, just as the the bandit leader, having finished off the last of Lea's bread, was polishing it off with huge gulps of milk taken from the cooler. With a loud belch, the immense body lumbered onto the porch as Tomás came galloping back, leading Freeman's horse.

"It is done, *jefe*. I brought his horse. He's not much bueno, but the gringo had a good saddle and gun!"

Carrasco nodded approval, "You did well, Tomás. Here we find nothing, as I expected. I feel it was the señora who met Gregorio in the creek yesterday, and now we know Billy Frank's wife and son are going west. That leaves those little girls. Hmm-mm, now where do you think they could be?"

"*Jefe*," replied the gunslinger, "there's a corral down by the creek here. Since one of them met Gregorio downstream in the same creek, might not the others have gone from there, also?"

"You are one smart hombre, Tomás!" Carrasco barked, "*Andale!* Let's go, amigos!" The raiders rushed to mount their horses and race to the corral by the creek — and there stood Crook.

"Aye-ee!" exclaimed Tomás to his boss as they came to a wild, rough stop. "Now *that* is a real *caballo*!"

"Sí! And that will be your reward for killing the gringo!" replied the munificent Carrasco.

"Gracias, *jefe*. Thank you for letting me have such a fine animal!" Tomás crowed as he jumped down from his mount and unsaddled it. He lowered his saddle to the ground and, in anticipation, grabbed a bosal that was hanging on a corral post.

"Come, my pretty one," the Mexican crooned as he opened the gate and deftly shut it with one hand, never taking his eyes from the glistening, streak-faced sorrel he approached. Crook didn't move, just shook his head up and down. Tomás walked right up to the horse and easily slipped the bosal over his head and the saddle onto his back while speaking to the envious vaqueros watching from outside the corral.

"He is not only a beauty, but he is also very gentle," boasted the proud new owner. "Will I not look grand when I ride to Carmelita's house? So grand that she will finally marry with me!"

The rough bunch broke into laughter, making ribald remarks about the beauteous Carmelita, as Tomás stepped into the stirrup and hoisted himself into the saddle.

The beautiful, gleaming sorrel didn't have a crooked streak on his face for nothing. He virtually exploded into motion. Caught completely off guard, Tomás was thrown hard to the ground after only three jumps, and the spectators jeered and laughed at their fallen comrade.

"Carmelita would really love you if she could see what a gran' *vaquero* you are," jeered one. "You call that *caballo* gentle?" scoffed another. "You ride like a girl!"

Tomás angrily stumbled to his feet and stomped toward the horse, which had stopped pitching immediately and stood, quietly watching his dispossessed rider.

This time warily watching the horse, Tomás turned Crook around, and as he carefully eased his body into the saddle he pulled the reins tight toward his body. His exuberant audience let out a loud roar, and before Tomás's seat hit the saddle, Crook was already lunging forward. With one jump, the horse sunfished into the corral fence. The fence shattered as the powerful animal fell, rolling the Mexican under him as he crashed through the wood.

The laughter abruptly turned to silence as the wild-eyed animal scrambled to regain his footing and did so, coming up with feet flying. He raced through the startled crew toward the creek, leaving among the broken boards his bloodied rider staring as if in surprise. A ragged shard of wood, some two inches wide and twenty inches long, had been driven through Tomás's midsection, impaling him with a thrust of instant death.

Watching from a woodpile some fifty yards distant, Feliz held both hands across his mouth to keep from laughing aloud. "Just as the señora said — one less to be sent to Hell," muttered the old Mexican, as his attention turned to Carrasco, who was barking out orders.

"Felipe! Juan! Go after that horse! And look for prints while you are down there!"

As the two riders left the stunned group, Carrasco spun on the next speechless man: "Gato, you take Pablo and Beto and go after the young woman and the boy." And as his anger grew, he shouted, "I don't care if you have to kill them—just get them! *Vamos! Andale!*" The three needed no urging; they mounted and rode away at a dead run.

The fat man's face was by now almost purple with rage as he grabbed the next henchman by the neck. "Manuel, like I told you last night, go to Gomez! Tell him he needs to wait no longer to cut!"

"Sí, señor," answered the Mexican, grateful for being let off so easy. Digging his spurs into his horse's side, he raced to the creek, reaching it as the first two were clambering out of the muddy bank on the far side. One of them turned and yelled, "*Jefe!* The tracks of two mules! Maybe the same as the animals the señora used in town yesterday!"

"Bueno!" Carrasco shouted back, "follow them, for they must be carrying the girls!" Turning to the last man at his side, "Follow the creek to where we found Gregorio's body. You will meet Chacón, who I sent last night to get the drunk gringo to check for footprints at first light. Pick up the trail of the old woman and kill her when you find her! I am going back to the trading post to await news from each of you." As the last man departed, Carrasco's voice rose, shouting after all of them, "Don't fail me, hombres, or you will wish you were dead as Tomás!"

With one step he mounted his horse and, with a disgusted last look at the backs of his departing men, jerked the horse around and thundered past the McKittrick house and onto the road leading back to the fort.

As the intruders disappeared in all directions, Feliz

remained silent and motionless in the woodpile. After a few minutes he crept out, ran toward the creek and crossed it, continuing on to a large copse of six-foot-high bee-brush that stood near the creek bank. The beloved old McKittrick ranchhand's heart beat wildly as he pushed through the sweet smell of the brush; seconds later he emerged, leading out a small red-and-white pony.

"Pinto," he gasped, "we must go fast but with much quiet to catch the hombre that rides to Gomez. Nothing more must happen to Señor Will and Billy Frank." Feliz scrambled onto the pony, and they moved quickly and silently along the route taken by the rider called Manuel.

/\.\/\/\.\/\

As first light of the gray dawn rose with the mist between the hills, the mother and son left the spring still gushing from its limitless aquifer. They followed its channel until it was split by a three-pronged outcropping of lava that made a natural escape for the water to flow in three different directions, leading to the valley below. There were neither trees nor mountains to obstruct the view, only a vast sea of grass cured to a golden wheat color at this time of year. Playing with the wind, the grass swayed to and fro; from the hills near Presidio on the south, it rippled northward for some hundred miles to stop abruptly at the base of the great Rockies. For all its scenic grandeur, the sea of grass was, by far, more dangerous to traverse than the high mountain peaks. It provided perfect cover for the prairie dog and his burrow and shade from the relentless sun for the diamondback rattlesnake. And, where the split occurred in the lava flow, water concealed dozens of small bluffs and caves. Wisely, Will had often advised, "Neither water nor valley do you cross, unless you know where you're going. To play it safe, just stay on the Overland Trail; you'll get to where you're going a lot faster, and you'll damn sure be a whole lot healthier!"

Carie well knew the risks involved in this route and had devised the best plan she could think of to minimize the danger to Lea and little Willie.

Therefore, as Lea and Willie drove the wagon only as far as the first slab of rock, Lea slammed on the brake, bringing Hit to a quick stop. They unhitched the red mule. Then, with little Willie mounted on Gran Carie's small but sturdy gray horse, they tied the lariat to the wagon bed and pulled it, causing it to capsize in the flowing stream. Lea then sliced up the mule harness to render it useless, and she and Willie made a game of throwing the leather pieces in after the now-floating wagon. When it reached the first small bluff, the wagon groaned as it smashed against the rocks. Its wreckage disappeared as it was sucked into a cave below.

Willie, with a smile so like his grandfather's, brushed his hands across his grandmother's jacket and pulled back the floppy beaver hat to reveal black curls that lay in disarray on his forehead. He sat down and, patting the rock next to him, beckoned his mother to do the same.

"Mama, Carrasco's sure not going to know where the wagon went and, even if he finds any of the leather from the harness, it won't be no use."

Lea's heart skipped a beat as she looked into his beautiful, laughing eyes.

"He'll not understand where the mule is, either, will he, Mama?"

"No, dear son, and that's our Gran Carie's scheme," said Lea, choking on a laugh she hoped would cover the growing fear for her man-child. "Now, up you go, son," she said, as she rose to pull him up. "Ride hard to the Jones Ranch and tell George what has happened. I'm sure he'll be more than willing to help you get to the little hill that's just above the road leading to Presidio. And your warning will give him plenty of time to protect his own spread, if any of the Carrasco renegades go that way. You have at least three days, Willie." Then, with her heart near the breaking point, she offered one last motherly admonition: "Willie, as your Gran Carie said to all of us, don't take any chances!"

Willie's handsome little face grew solemn and, with his chest swelling with the pride of approaching manhood, he said, "Don't worry, Mama, I'll do everything just like you told me." Then, again reverting to the child, he said quietly, "I love you, Mama." As the last words slipped out, he spun the gray pony, racing off and over the hill toward the Jones' ranch.

Lea clasped her arms around her body and shuddered. The tears, so long suppressed, began to flow down her cheeks; she watched the departing figure of her only son until horse and rider reached the horizon. Then she reached down to pick up Hit's rein, now shortened for riding, jumped to throw her body across the mule's back, then wriggled to seat herself. When she clucked to the mule to get going, the big red suddenly brayed, so startling Lea that she momentarily forgot her troubles. She whacked the mule hard with the rein across his hip, scolding, "You damned old fool! If I can bear being alone and separated from my loved ones, so can you!" Hit complied by stepping out to a fast, swaying trot, his tail wagging like a dog's.

/\\\\/\\\\

Willie made good time over the low hills and valleys that led to the Jones' spread. Chance was a wonderful horse to ride, for he had been both expertly and patiently trained by Carie herself during the long war years. Though he was much smaller than his Thoroughbred brothers, he had the breed's great stamina and heart and always reached out to match his gait to theirs. At a hundred yards there were none that could outrun him, but for the distance, the longer-legged horses with their slim bodies and long gaskins would pass him by. But Chance was quicker, therefore was the best cutter, and, by the same standard, was the best calf-roping horse. He could catch a calf before the animal knew the horse was even near. His most spectacular trait was such a smooth ride that Carie could not only shoot from the little gray, but, racing over a hill or into brush to catch a shot at a running deer, she was given a better than even chance to down the fleet animal within two hundred yards.

So, it was the fault of neither the boy nor the horse that just as the sun reached its cloudy zenith, both were in the wrong place at the wrong time.

Manuel, sent by his *jefe* with the message to Gomez

at Rustlers' Cave, decided he'd make a small detour to take his noontime *comida*. As his empty stomach started him thinking of food, he rationalized that it would be to the *jefe's* advantage to know what those Jones gringos might be up to. Not only that, his horse needed watering, and both would feel much better after a short rest under the cottonwoods at the Jones place. He was therefore much surprised when he saw the slight figure on the gray pony within a mile of the ranch house. Thinking it was the señora, Manuel reined to a quick stop. He dismounted and, not bothering to tie his tired horse, pulled his rifle from its scabbard, squatted, and fired one shot. Willie was untouched, but Chance caught the bullet in the neck. Both horse and rider tumbled, end over end.

As the Mexican rose, grinning at his trophy, a second shot rang out. Manuel dropped in his tracks, blood spurting from a head nearly shot off. His horse fled the scene and, from the opposite direction, the oncoming Feliz barely avoided colliding with him as their paths crossed. Feliz sped onward, spurring the little paint hard to reach the small, motionless body.

Feliz reined the now-crazed horse to a stop and, looking aghast at the stilled horse and boy said, "*Por Dios*, not our little one!" For an instant transfixed, Feliz could not move his eyes from Willie's crumpled form. Then, with a look of disbelief, he lept from the paint, yelling. "He lives! *Mira*! My friend, he lives!" The paint spooked and lurched backwards, yanking Feliz's arm. "Stop, you loco bastard!" shouted the old man, and the horse stood still as Feliz rushed to the child's side.

The precious little face, so like his grandfather Will,

was now covered with dirt, and a large, blue bruise was appearing around his right eye. When Willie began to stir, his first awareness was the embracing arms of the old Mexican and the next sensation was that every bone in his body was in pain.

In a voice husky with emotion, the old man said, "*Mijo*, don't move. You'll feel better in a minute."

Willie groaned, "I — I don't think so — ugh, oh-h-hhh," as he tried to focus through his rapidly swelling and puffed eyes. Then, unable to believe what he saw, he looked squarely into the eyes of old Feliz and said, "Where in hell did you come from?"

Feliz howled like a coyote, and Willie found he could actually grin without much pain.

Feliz picked up the boy and hugged him close to his body, murmuring softly against his dusty hair, "I will never ask The Great One for another thing in this life. He has given me yours."

Willie couldn't answer. He stared in horror over Feliz's shoulder, his eyes riveted to the sight of the stilled body of Chance, Gran Carie's brave little gray.

∧·∨·∧

Astride the placid mule, Lea plodded along the Overland Trail which led through the vast valley toward Adobe Wells. Never stopping, she took sips of water and nibbled on a biscuit to ease the gnawing pangs of hunger. Heading northward, she felt the brisk, cold wind increasing, but the tall grasses acted as something of a windbreak. She hugged the sheepskin brush jacket close to her body and was fairly comfortable. That is, she thought, if anyone *could* be comfortable riding a mule. She was instantly ashamed as she thought of Carie's long ride on Hammer.

While the mule's rocking gait seemed slow, in reality he provided quite a good way to travel. Like the proverbial tortoise and hare, Hit swayed along steadily and in pretty good time. Therefore, it was mid-afternoon when Lea arrived at Adobe Wells.

Adobe Wells wasn't a town; it was simply a lone, mudhut stagecoach stop. It was deserted; not even an animal of any kind occupied its dreary-looking round-pole corral.

Oh, well, she thought, *it's just as well that no one is here. I'm too tired and much too worried to have to talk to anyone. All I want to do right now is wash up and fix something to eat. After that, I'll go and get things ready, just in case I have visitors.*

Then remembering that she already had a companion, she reached down to pat the mule's sweat-crusted hide. "Golly, Hit, I almost forgot about you." Dismounting, she led the tired animal to the corral and removed his headgear. The big red dropped his head gratefully into the water trough and, with great gulping sounds, drank his fill. Lea crossed to the lean-to that served as a shelter for animals. From a wooden box she scooped up a bucketful of grain and poured it into the trough. Hit brayed once, and then again, even louder. Lea grinned and her expression softened; the inherent gentleness returned to her voice as she said, "You're welcome, Hit, and I thank you, too."

The quiet, pleasant thoughts were to be short-lived, for the three men sent by Carrasco to find her arrived at dusk. Arrogantly they sat on their scrawny mounts just looking, and Lea's long-eared mule looked back. They had brazenly ridden up to the mud hut, expecting to easily overpower the beautiful woman (their first mistake). They were gleefully deciding just which of them would be first to sample the delights of her luscious body. Lea, however, was ready for them. What the rough bunch had not bargained for was Billy Frank's training of his wife in self- protection. Lea was a crack shot with a shotgun. In fact, none of the McKittrick men could match the skill of this quiet, patient woman when it came to birds. She could down a covey of quail before Will or Billy Frank could even bag one or two. Her shotgun, held firmly to her shoulder, would thunder away; when it fell silent, it was only because she had sufficient for the family's evening meal. She'd pick up her fat little catch of quail and, winking at Carie as she passed, would calmly walk back to the house. Big Will would howl with laughter, while Billy Frank could only manage a weak smile.

The blast from Lea's first shell caught Pablo squarely in the midsection; the second hit the shoulder of the man named Gato. Beto fled, deciding that life in El Paso would be much healthier. His wounded amigos thought so, too, and they all rapidly headed north on the Overland Trail.

This was to be their second (and worst) mistake.

5

VVVVVV

The Horses

ON THE OTHER SIDE of the mountains, to the east, Meri and High Cloud were already moving their charges.

The day had begun with the sun trying to penetrate the heavy clouds. A strong southern wind came to its rescue and began to blow the miserable sleet-laden clouds to the east and north, leaving a wonderland of melting ice and the promise of a perfect fall day.

High Cloud had spent a restless night, for he knew what the bandits' reaction would be when they found the body of Gregório. When Meri awakened to the heavenly smell of coffee and frying bacon, High Cloud told her he was going to take care of his own horses, as well as hers. This was the truth, but he hedged about the time required to do it. He had already spent the early hours before daybreak feeding and inspecting each of the horses. After the animals had eaten their fill, High Cloud had saddled Stretch for Meri and the strong, durable Fargo for himself.

Blissfully unaware of High Cloud's worries, Meri treated herself to a hearty breakfast and again luxuriated in a soaking bath in the wooden tub. She smoothed the healing salve on the abrasions on her body and the wounds on her hands and wrists and then set about readying for their departure. Being so much like her mother, not only in appearance, but also in so many character traits, Meri was a perfectionist. She repacked both her own and High Cloud's saddle bags with a change of clean clothes and, in the space remaining, stuffed the prepared food. Satisfied that they had all they could carry, she deftly made up the bed and began to tidy up the little dugout.

So it was that when High Cloud caught the first glimpse of distant riders coming around the bend in the pass, he and Meri were ready to leave at a moment's notice.

"Meri," he called out as he opened the door, "Carrasco's men are coming through the pass! We must go NOW!"

"I'm ready," she answered, hastily drawing on her leggings and brush jacket.

High Cloud crossed to the table and looked in his pouch to see what Meri had packed for him, then word-lessly closed it. Picking up both pouches with one great hand, he grabbed two Navajo blankets from the bed as Meri jammed on her battered hat and followed him through the door. Outside, they darted around the dugout to the pole corral where Stretch and Fargo waited patiently.

When Meri was mounted, High Cloud spoke rapidly as he tied her saddle bag and blanket on the back of the cantle. "No need to carry your rifle, just leave it in the scabbard. We'll ease the horses out in the open, and we'll be in plain sight. Then we'll wait 'til those hombres get within a mile of us."

Meri frowned questioningly, but High Cloud continued outlining his strategy. "They're tired. They've already come a long way, which means their horses will also be tired—and thirsty. I want them to see us, and I want those dumb *gentes* to think they have an advantage."

High Cloud grinned broadly as he saw the dawn of understanding light up Meri's face. "In other words," he continued, "I want to force them to pursue us without stopping here to water their mounts and rest. On the other hand, our ponies are rested and fit. We'll stay just far enough ahead to keep them in pursuit. By the time they get to the next water at San Solomon Springs, they will have no choice—they will have to stop. I will stop when they do, enticing them to make their rest seem more worthwhile. You will go on toward San Martine."

Meri, unable to contain herself, laughed aloud and leaned down from her high perch to plant a kiss on the young brave's cheek, saying "Spoken like Grandpa Will!" Before the abashed High Cloud could answer,

Meri expertly opened the corral gate and whistled to the horses.

And so it was: as the men neared, Meri on Stretch was at "point" near the end of the bluff, leading only the irascible Pretty Boy. The sleek geldings followed, their heads above those of the younger two- and three-year-olds. High Cloud took his position at the rear, and they waited.

It was quite a sight to see—a bunch of totally stupid men racing their exhausted mounts across the valley in futile pursuit. When the pursuers had reached the prescribed point, Meri gently moved her reins to the left, touched Stretch lightly with her spurs, and, whistling to the herd, set out at a slow trot.

During the next two hours—even at that slow pace —Chacón, his Latino brother, and the somewhat sober but oh-so-very-sick gringo were never able to close the gap. Their poor mounts stumbled with exhaustion; the pale, white Charlie begged to be left to die where he fell. Chacón, thoroughly disgusted with the whole affair, flung Charlie across the saddle of his pitiful steed and declared he himself would put a bullet through Charlie's pickled brain if he didn't shut up.

The air was crisp and fresh, and as the horses passed the last hill, the sparkle of the sun on the lake fed by San Solomon Springs and the vast plain beyond came into view. Meri clucked to Stretch, and the bay instantly responded with a slow lope. Within minutes the horses covered the last mile to water. Meri let the animals drink their fill, and with High Cloud's help, headed the herd toward the north. As they crossed a small arroyo, High Cloud stopped and gave a shrill whistle. Meri knew the signal meant High Cloud was staying there, according to plan. She never turned in her saddle to look back, just waved her hand in reply and moved on.

The expected happened. The now completely demoralized and disheveled pursuers could see the herd, now on the horizon. Upon seeing the lake and the stage house on its far side, they chose to discontinue pursuit and instead stopped for "a quick drink of the *cerveza*, and *agua* for the *caballos*." Inside the stage house, the unsuspecting bandidos drank and griped and drank some more. Even as they drank, High Cloud rode up and boldly untethered their horses, calmly leading them to a nearby stream that led away from the main body of water—a body of water that gushed up to form a lake two miles wide and four miles long that lay in a bed of solid lava rock at the base of the mountains. High Cloud unsaddled the horses, then cut the girths from the saddles; the bridles were granted equal treatment, and he tossed the men's sorry blankets into the water. Smiling with satisfaction, he mounted and loped off toward the now-distant Meri and the herd.

Discovering their horses gone, Chacón and his dispirited compadres rushed out into the wagon yard, only to see their animals grazing almost half a mile distant. When the men splashed through the stream to catch the horses, a soggy Charlie spied bits of their slashed tack floating merrily away. Saddles were scarce in Texas, and it was all just too much for Chacon's addled brain to withstand. He straggled back to the bank and collapsed. He had had all he could take and, as he passed the hapless gringo, he gave him a swift kick and proclaimed loudly, "I'm goin' to catch the next stage east instead of west!"

With this happy thought, Charlie jumped to his feet with renewed vigor and shouted, "Aw right! Now, how 'bout another beer?"

/\.\/.\/\.\

Meri and High Cloud caught sight of their destination as they rounded the northern end of the Davis Mountains. Riding just below Texas' fourth-highest peak, Meri looked down upon some of the most desolate terrain she had ever seen. Far to the northwest, across an ancient, hundred-mile-long alkaline sea, the majestic Guadalupes stood like ghostly monks. Below the riders, the rolling Red Hills, where San Martine Spring was one of the last places on the trail to El Paso that one could get good water. This area marked the last really productive land for ninety miles in any direction. Its red hills are aptly named for the clay that mixed with ash from ancient craters and rich, black humus that had found its way down from the mountains. The sharp red rock that covered the hills was blanketed with rich gama grass but only sparsely sprinkled with a few cedars at high points and creek willow that nestled in the canyons between. Probably the best thing that could be said about this area was that it was easier to traverse than the mountains—for man and beast alike. Consequently it held some of the largest mule deer in Texas, which drew all races of men to the area for the rich meat. Therein stood the danger, as men fought for control of the riches of water and food.

Stretch spied Carie even before Meri did, and he nick-

ered. Old Hammer brayed in response. With a yelp of
joy, Meri spurred Stretch into a run—down, then across,
and up again to the next ridge, High Cloud and the
geldings eagerly following.

"Gran Carie, we made it!" Meri yelled, flinging herself into her grandmother's waiting arms. "What a surprise, to find you already here!" She hugged the little
woman seated on her huge mule.

"Made good time," replied Carie, as High Cloud
pulled to a stop at her side. "My son," the tiny woman
said to the brave, her sparkling gray eyes looking deeply
into his amber ones, "I thank you."

The young man's face betrayed the swelling of understood emotion, but he answered quietly, "You're most
welcome, Gran Carie."

"Well, then," Carie said, smiling her approval at the
two, "let's get this good-looking bunch settled in your
grandfather's camp, High Cloud, before dark. Then
you, young lady, can tell me what's been going on," eye-
ing the yellowed bruise on Meri's cheek. Before the girl
could answer, Carie spurred Hammer down the hill and
headed toward a stand of hackberry and willow near the
spring. Through the trees, smoke could be seen curling
from the tepees—White Cloud's camp.

As they approached, a majestic old Indian clad in
worn buckskins, a lone feather waving from the back of
his gray head, strode from the camp and raised his hand
in salute. "Welcome, Gran Carie, and our sister, Meri."

"You look well, White Cloud," Carie responded. But
Meri didn't stand on ceremony and jumped down from
Stretch to fling her arms around his thin body, just as
she had done to Carie.

Only then did the leathered face break into a warm and genuine smile. He patted her shoulders. Then, stepping back from the young girl, his face again changed to its usual stoic expression as his brilliant black eyes alighted upon High Cloud.

"And welcome to you, Grandson."

The handsome young man dropped his head in respectful deference and replied quietly, "It is with much joy I am again in your presence, Grandfather."

The old Indian nodded in agreement, and turned again to Carie. "Your horses will be safe in the box canyon beyond the hill of the spring."

"Thank you, White Cloud, but there are—" and before she could finish, the two hundred-plus mares and colts came thundering into view, with Missy at the lead, waving wildly.

"You brought the whole herd," White Cloud said in wonderment.

"Yes," Carie replied, "it's a long story." To the young people at her side, Carie added quickly, "Get the geldings out of the way before Skye's Son gets here, or we'll have a battle on our hands. Best you take them below the camp; hobble 'em to graze. We can put the mares and colts in the box canyon."

There was not time, however, for the fleet Thoroughbreds were too fast, and Carie had to run to catch Skye's Son. The small band of Apaches—three old men, five elderly women and a young girl, all that remained of White Cloud's once-proud tribe—came running out to help with the animals. It was complete havoc, with bites and kicks for all offenders, nickers and brays from mothers to their young, with squeals and pawing, until Carie, in frustration, asked the old chief if he had any corn to spare.

White Cloud was pleased that he could be of help to restore order, and he trotted off with one of the other men to get the grain.

Only when the last morsel had been poured out on the ground, did peace again come to the little camp— that is, until Missy came in on a cloud of dust. Old Alice gracefully came to a sliding stop just inches from Carie, Boots barking at her heels, and her black colt's wild eyes peering from behind its mother.

"Meri! High Cloud! I saw you from the hill as you came in, and I'm so glad to see you!" Typical of the animated youngster, never taking a breath, her voice rose to an even higher pitch as her flashing eyes flitted from one to another of her loved ones. "Whattaya think of the Ranger?" she asked, pointing to Mona's rider as he stepped down from the mare's side. "He buried ole Bird Man after he got kilt by a blind rattler, but I made him my pris'ner, 'cause he was a Reb, but he didn't shoot Pa's leg off, and I guess he's a fren' now, 'cause he's gonna help us go get Pa and Grandpa Will—isn't that just wonderful?" Pausing as if she expected at least one of the group to answer, she caught her breath. Then, unable to contain her impatience at the dumb-struck group, she positively howled, "Well, why in the hell doesn't somebody SAY something!"

Clearing her throat to suppress a chuckle, Carie assumed a stern voice as she said, "I'll say something, Missy. I'm going to wash your mouth out with soap!"

John Revell gasped, "I've been wanting to do that for two days!" and gave way to a fit of laughter.

Meri's soft doe-eyes never left the face of the Ranger, as if she had never seen a man before. Her rapt attention to John Revell did not escape the notice of High Cloud; his eyes suddenly shadowed over in sadness, and he turned away to stride toward the camp. Carie gazed in silence at the departing back of High Cloud, then said, "Ranger, this is Meredith, my other granddaughter."

The impetuous and unpredictable Missy, sighting a distant, golden-coated animal approaching, yelled, "Duke!" and slid off Alice, tossing the reins to her startled grandmother. Missy fairly flew down the hill to her Palomino. This caused John Revell to laugh even harder, bringing tears to his eyes. He turned, still laughing, to look into Meri's lovely, smiling face framed by auburn hair falling across her shoulders in a cascade of bewitching curls. It took his breath away. He choked, swallowed hard and opened his mouth to speak, but could not.

The girl's soft brown eyes sparkled as she timidly reached out to touch a tear on his cheek. This gentle act of kindness undid the poor man, and he could only stammer, "Wha—"

Sensing that she might have made a monumental blunder, Meri flushed as she said, "I'm sorry, it's just that I never saw a man cry before."

Along with curious warmth, John had an unexpected sense of peace. "They're tears of joy. Your little sister is just about the most...." But he was unable to continue, and he just stood there foolishly grinning at the lovely girl.

"I know," she whispered in reply, her eyes meeting his in perfect understanding.

The chill dusk found the weary travelers huddled

around a flickering campfire, trading stories of their individual adventures during the last two days, Carie's solemn eyes moving to each in turn. There were mixed emotions as Meri related her narrow escape, but laughter prevailed when Missy proudly narrated her capture of "the pris'ner."

However, it was Carie who brought home the purpose of their being here and now, and they listened intently as the little woman laid out her plan. "Tomorrow's going to be a day of rest, but we've still some work to do. Meri, I want you to check all of the supplies, and, with the Ranger's help, pack all we can load onto old Hammer. High Cloud and I, and Missy," she continues, her sharp gray eyes glancing to meet Missy's, "we'll separate the colts from the mares, and we'll leave behind only the oldest mares to mother the youngest colts for now. Then," she explained, smiling at the old Indian by her side, "White Cloud will tend to them, and in about a week's time he'll move them back to the ranch. We should be home with your Papa and Grandpa Will by that time!"

The last words brought cheers and whoops. The Indian braves summoned the gods to raise them to their feet and slowly began to dance around the campfire and chant.

This was too much for the ebullient Missy; she sprang to her feet and joined the ritual, and one by one the others followed, their voices mingling with those of their brothers.

/\\.\\/\\.\\/\\

Will's dream transported him and brought an incredible feeling of comforting warmth to his aching left hand. In his sleep, a moan of well-being escaped his lips, instantly silenced by a rough hand over his mouth. His eyes flew open and blinked rapidly as he tried to shake off sleep. Gradually he saw through the murky predawn light that crept into the cave and could make out the face of the filthy Chinese cook only inches from his own face. The man had one finger raised to his lips to signal silence. The slanted yellow eyes never left the big man as he slowly, ever so slowly, withdrew his hand. Rapidly but carefully he removed the crude bandage from Will's hand, then wrapped it with a steaming hot rag.

"Oh, Gawd, that feels good," he whispered. "Smells like the devil, but I don't care. What did you put on it?" There was no answer; only a wide smile that revealed a toothless mouth.

The laugh lines around Will's black eyes deepened, and his inherent sense of the ridiculous caused him to cough in spasms to prevent his laughing aloud.

The sound caused Billy Frank, huddled in a knot at Will's side, to stir, and whisper, "What's th' matter, Pa?"

"Everything's just fine, son," was the hushed reply, and he raised his newly bandaged hand for Billy Frank to see. "The Chinaman just doctored my hand, and it sure feels better."

"Wonder why. I guess he has no love lost for our top rooster," Billy Frank chuckled while rubbing his grizzled face. He stretched, slowly, to ease the kinks out of his cramped, aching body.

The poorly-clad cook had soundlessly slipped through the gloom to the campfire but shortly returned with two steaming cups of coffee and a large, round piece of camp bread with slabs of venison tucked inside. He squatted to hand the food to Will and Billy Frank, and his worn little face again broke into a wide, conspiratorial grin. The two hungry men wolfed down the food, neither speaking until the last dregs of coffee were consumed. Sighing with contentment, Will reached out to touch the man's shoulder and whispered, "My thanks, friend, but why put yourself in harm's way to help us?"

When no answer came from the grinning face, Will persisted.

"What's your name, feller? 'Tis one I'll never want to forget."

The cook, rising to his feet, leaned over the two men. He opened his mouth wide, revealing not only that he had no teeth, but he also had no tongue.

"Gawd, Pa, we have no problems a'tall compared to this pore feller," Billy Frank hissed in horror.

Will's sharp jaw clenched ad he growled, "Son, when we get out of here, if it's the last thing I do it'll be to help this good man." One man's black eyes were brittle hard, the other's thoughtful. "That's a promise, Billy Frank."

"A promise we'll keep, Pa," was the quiet reply.

Father and son, now sustained by food and the warmth of hot coffee, again huddled close together. They watched intently as the now distant figure of the mute cook moved around the campfire preparing breakfast for the outlaws.

.\.\.\.\.

Far to the north, in the camp by the spring, Carie's

crew was already hard at work. The Ranger marveled that the elderly lady could move so fast in assigning chores to each person. He decided she somehow had the instincts and talents of an army general. By the time the sun neared its zenith, the designated mares had been led quietly out of the trap by Carie, Missy, and High Cloud. Then, together, the Ranger and Meri eased them away to the small valley near the spring to feed upon the lush, tall grass.

There had been not a single hitch in the process, until old White Cloud, who had been manning the gate, suggested it might be wise to leave Pretty Boy behind because his ankle had swollen even more from the previous day's flight.

Meri glared her unspoken disapproval, but Carie agreed with White Cloud. "No, Meri, he's right. We can't risk taking any horse that isn't fit for the trip. Pretty Boy will be safe here, but I'm just not so sure how safe the others we leave behind will be from his hind feet!" They all laughed.

Tension melted as the decision was accepted. The colts were separated from their mothers, and in their play could be heard the sounds of a squeal as one nipped at another or the plaintive nickers of the mares as they left their colts.

Even though it's time, and the mares know it, thought Carie.

As the afternoon shadows lengthened, Meri inspected every item of clothing the group had and carefully packed the tarps full. As the last rays of the sun set, she packed as much of the food supplies as could be carried. John Revell was constantly at her side, helping without being asked and relishing each smile and thank you that came his way from the girl. Only when the last pack was securely tied in readiness for Hammer's back did the two stop and gaze into each other's eyes. This time it was the large hand that trembled to touch that of the young girl, and the deep, masculine voice shook as he said, "You're special."

/\/\/\

So, Carie thought, *by Gomez's calculation, it was the fourth day since the more than two hundred horses had started their run across forty miles of the arid, cold country.* Carie seldom allowed the horses to walk, instead taking them to either a lope or a trot. As she explained to the Ranger, "You can walk a horse down real quick, but it takes days to trot or run him down. These horses are fit, full of water and good, rich, mountain grass; so, with a stop every two hours, by first dark we should be at the ridge of the Delawares."

With High Cloud at left point, Carie at right point, Meri and Missy on either side as flankers, and John bringing up drag, more than eight hundred hoofs started to move west. The sound was unbelievable: hoofs clanging against rock, and thudding on turf at different cadences, nostrils blowing and, adding to the din, the ever-ridiculous bray from Hammer, who followed Ranger John and Boots at drag.

While the sound was indeed incredible, the *sight* of the horses was even more breathtaking. The stark white of the alkali terrain seemed to set off the colors of the horses vividly.

Like my grandfather's ceremonial dress, thought High Cloud, remembering the bleached doeskin adorned by the multicolored beading so intricately hand-worked throughout the garment—from the chest to the fringed trouser legs.

It was a joy to see the horses at a trot, with their sculptured, noble heads, necks arched, slim legs lifting up and down in a delicate prance. At a run, these majestic Thoroughbreds rivaled the beauty of any living creature. They were grace in motion, with mane and tail lifting and falling to the cadence of each step, their necks reaching forward as their legs stretched, ligaments and tendons strained to their limits. Any observer would realize that no other animal could contain a heart large enough to put forth such valiant, sustained effort.

It was this valiant effort Carie had counted on at the time she decided to go west, straight over the Delawares instead of going around them. Coming from the eastern side, the land remained flat. The western side was quite a different matter, and most travelers chose another route. Approaching from the east, you were already atop the crest of a 6500-foot-high mountain, without having to climb it. It was awesome to look down onto the great Salt Flat below (five to seven miles away, as the crow flies), only 1500 feet above sea level. Try to imagine climbing *down* the face of that bluff: the mountains drop off abruptly into four or five ever-widening ledges, all the way down to the valley floor. One might view the sheer drop and say, "There's no way I'm going to be able to get down there safely," or, "You can't get there from here." It was the roughest and most dangerous terrain in West Texas.

Carie herself had, as many have done, gone down the bluff as well as up, following trails no broader than a horse's hoof; trails made by deer and other wildlife that abounded in that environment. But she had no doubt about which route to take. The shortest distance to Salt Flat was a straight line, saving one full day of travel time. They reached the crest before dusk, and Mother Nature blessed them with not only clear skies but a vivid orange, red, and yellow-streaked sunset. Feeling at one with nature, Carie marveled at the delicate balance of power, give and take, the danger of the harsh land versus its productivity and beauty.

This panoramic view was the backdrop for the fire that John Revell built for their evening meal. Meri and High Cloud unsaddled the mounts, lovingly gave each a rubdown, then hobbled them to graze. Missy, along with the loyal Boots, took first watch over the herd. The animals were allowed to spread out and nose along the rocky crests for ancient potholes painstakingly ground out by Indians centuries ago to catch rainwater. This was a dry stop; precious water was some five miles distant, down in the flat.

Carie unburdened Hammer and staked him nearby, for the mares had no use for the mule and less tolerance for him. This task done, Carie whistled for Skye's Son, who had not been ridden all day. The stallion immediately came to her side. She patted his majestic forehead while slipping a grass halter over his head, and, speaking softly, told him, "I hate to do this to you, old boy, but if you're quiet the herd will be, too." She staked him near the fire, next to her own saddle and gear. The beans and bread brought from San Martine were devoured, and as the fresh, hot coffee was downed, High Cloud left to relieve Missy. When the little girl arrived at the camp, John hobbled Missy's horse for the night. Darkness descended, and bright stars twinkled at those below. Meri saw to it that her little sister was fed and afterward tucked into a blanket, with a saddle as a pillow. With Boots curled up at her side, the tired little Missy was asleep even as her eyes closed. Minutes later, Carie joined her, but lay looking up at the clear night sky, mentally going over every step of the descent they would make on the morrow.

John and Meri walked to the edge of the crest and gazed down at the Salt Flat outpost, now evident because of the distant campfires at the military camp. Few words had been spoken on this evening; tasks assigned had been carried out automatically. John broke the silence. "We'd best turn in, too, Meri, for I stand watch at midnight." As the pair joined the little one in sleep, Carie's gray eyes continued to gaze at the stars.

Next morning, when everything stood in readiness—campfire cold and covered, gear packed, herd gathered—all the riders mounted expectantly.

"We must wait 'til full sun before starting down; I want everyone to be able to see exactly where they're stepping," Carie said to the silent but alert group. "We'll split into two groups. Skye's Son and I take the right-handed ridge with the geldings and some of the younger, braver mares. The Ranger and Hammer follow last."

They all looked blank, for they could see no downward trail.

Carie continued. "High Cloud and Alice will take the

left ridge. Look," she said, pointing to the jagged trail roughly carved out of rock and stone, "now that the sun is out, you can see a distinct trail, clear down to the bottom."

This time, all the nods were affirmative; all, that is, except for the Ranger, John Revell. He could do nothing but stare downward in disbelief.

"All the mares will just naturally follow Alice, so with a little urging from Meri and Missy, who will be last, there should be none that refuse to follow." Then, as she was carefully examining each face to see if all understood, there was a chorus from them: "Yes, ma'am."

With no further need for words, Carie and the great stallion took the first steps. She never looked back but went carefully stepping, slipping, sliding, over the point of the shelf. Cautiously, the other horses followed, emulating the leader. One by one, the geldings crossed the point. Due to the gentle persuasion of High Cloud, the young mares hesitated but a little. Then the older mares that had been hand-picked from the herd by Meri and Missy began to step downward onto the narrow shelf.

As they had watched from the crest, no words had been exchanged between John and High Cloud, but as the Indian passed John and the smaller group of horses, each nodded good luck to the other. The Indian lightly tapped the gray lead mare Alice's side and moved out, the other mares followed, urged onward by the shrill whistles from the girls.

After the last mare had moved down, the girls and their mounts finally went over the crest. Only then did John Revell follow Carie, who by this time was disappearing from view over the second shelf-ridged mountain, some 1,000 feet below. With his mount's first step over the side, John realized what this remarkable woman had planned.

Carie had assumed the greatest risk of them all, by going first on an unmarked trail and, not only that, but taking with her the horses that would be the most diffi-cult to control. Considering High Cloud to be the sec-ond-most knowledgeable horseman, Carie had put him in charge of the quiet, cautious mares. The girls, follow-ing these cautious beasts, were placed by Carie in the only position that could have been even remotely con-sidered "safe" or "protected."

The Ranger had been placed last. In this decision, Carie's experience, her knowledge of the terrain, and of her horses were the trump cards. She must have decided that he was the only person who would give his all if any one of the others was hurt, or, greater yet, the only per-son who would take charge if anything happened to Carie. The Ranger's heart swelled. She trusted him.

Some three hours later, after having followed the haz-ardous trail an incredible 4,500 feet lower, Carie sat calmly on a large, flat rock on the last small hill before the final descent into the valley that held the briny salt lake. In a ravine below the hill, High Cloud tended all of her horses and two thirds of his. All was quiet as she watched the last thirty mares cautiously make their way down.

On the adjacent mountain, John Revell was in almost a direct line of sight with the girls when the golden Duke, carrying Missy, lost his footing and fell. Two things saved the child. First, the girls were on the last and lowest shelf, also the flattest, although there was yet a 200-foot drop to the canyon below. Second, and more important, was her training. From the time they first handled a horse, the children had been told that, "If your horse should fall, try to fling your body *away* from his. In the case of being on a mountain trail, fall *toward* the mountain; don't let the horse pull you over the cliff."

So it was, that when Duke slipped and started falling, Missy instinctively threw her small body toward the mountain. Landing hard on the rocky tier and scratching with both hands for something to cling to, she dug her feet in for a perilous stand. With no way to halt his momentum, the beautiful little Duke was doomed. Over and down the mountainside he fell.

Stunned, and powerless to help, Carie and John watched as Meri eased Stretch beside Missy and leaned anxiously over the child, "Missy, how bad are you hurt?"

Terrified eyes met hers, trying in vain to blink back the tears streaming down her face. "I'm okay. My shoulder just hurts a little," Missy whimpered. Then sobbing, her hands cupping her eyes, over and over she wailed, "Oh, my poor Duke!"

"Enough!" Meri pleaded, "Enough, now. Can you get on your feet?"

The dusty, tear-streaked little face finally looked up at her sister, and Missy shuddered as she nodded in reply.

"All right! Get up, put your foot in my stirrup and swing up behind me." Cautiously, the child moved to Stretch's side and did so. When Missy assured her sister that she was set, Meri clucked to her mount and he resumed his slow descent down the narrow trail.

John was waiting beside the anxious Carie when the

two girls finally reached them. Tears still streamed down Missy's face as she slid into Revell's outstretched arms. She clung to the man and muttered, "Thank you, Johnny Reb." Tears welled in the Ranger's own eyes as the little girl turned to face her grandmother.

"Oh, Gran Carie, I kilt my pony! I'm so sorry! I kilt my pony! I didn't mean to, Gran Carie, honest!"

With great emotion showing in every line of her weathered face, Carie reached out with a trembling hand and brushed the tears from Missy's cheeks. "You didn't kill Duke, Missy. He just happened to step on a slick rock and lost his balance. Not having any way to regain it, he couldn't help but fall." The hand steadied and grasped the child's chin. "Now tell me where you hurt."

"It's jus' my shoulder," the child said, hiccupping, "but it only hurts a li'l bit."

Satisfied, Carie quickly mounted the stallion. "If you're sure you can make it to the Salt Flat Outpost, which won't take but about another thirty minutes, you can ride behind me on Skye's Son." The little girl nodded and held out her arms as the Ranger deftly lifted her behind her grandmother. It was then Carie noticed that Meri, whose face seemed to have aged ten years in the last twenty minutes, was gazing deeply into the compassionate eyes of the man. Carie patted the child's hands as they reached around her waist and quickly turned her horse before Missy could see High Cloud moving up the narrow canyon toward the mangled and torn body of the Palomino.

The herd needed no urging to start moving again. In fact, they were getting fidgety and irritated with one another, having been without water for so many hours.

The riders had their hands full on the way to the out-post. Picking up the scent of water, the horses began to run. John moved up front to help, certainly no longer needed at drag.

As the outpost came into view they could see a mounted cavalryman racing toward the thundering herd, waving a red cloth and yelling, "Stop! Stop! Y'all cain't bring all them hosses in hyeah!"

You don't tell a thirsty horse to stop, be it male or female, after such a long and arduous trip. The red banner served only to encourage the tired animals to run even faster—ears back, nostrils flaring—straight for the hapless trooper. When the soldier saw that he was in imminent danger of being run down by the stampede, he lost all reason and jerked his horse so cruelly that the animal reared, tossing its rider to the ground. Luckily, John raced to the addled soldier and pulled him onto his own mount before the herd could run him down.

"I'm thankin' ya, suh," croaked the voice of the man behind him.

"No trouble at all," answered the ex-Confederate officer, not in the least surprised that the cavalryman was black, a "buffalo soldier." What did surprise him, however, was that the huge man was a sergeant.

The entire McKittrick crew had its work cut out for them trying to restrain the scuffling horses scrambling to drink their fill from the twenty-foot trough. Carie had all she could do, holding onto Missy, controlling the black stallion, and seeing that each animal had its share of the precious liquid. She concentrated so intently on the horses that she ignored everything else. But Missy was seeing everything else, and now the little girl yelled above the din, "Gran Carie! There's a so'jer over there that's been hollering at you for ten minutes, and he shore looks mad!"

Sure enough, on the porch of the outpost's lone building stood an officer shaking his fist and yelling, but his words were undiscernible.

"Well, Missy," the little woman replied drily, "best we go see what the military is so upset about." Carie calmly walked Skye's Son over to the officer. As she approached, she could see perspiration cascading down the enraged man's reddened face; over and over he slapped his blue cavalry hat against his thigh.

He yelled even louder, "I demand to know what you think you are doing, watering all those damned horses here, when everyone knows we have to haul it all the way from Adobe Wells!" His face now almost purple, he continued, "And I'm going to put you under arrest for disobeying the sergeant I sent to stop you and causing him to be thrown—uh."

He stopped short as Carie removed her hat and nonchalantly wiped her brow on her sleeve. "Gawd! Uh—ah—oh, pardon me, ma'am, I didn't know you were a woman!"

Not only the fact that the doffed hat revealed a woman but Carie's eyes, turned pure steel, jerked the officer back to the reality that he was "an officer and a gentleman." Cordially now, he said, "Lieutenant Raymond Yancy at your service. Please come in, ma'am, and little lady, and be my guests for some refreshment after your long ride."

As Carie and the almost too-silent Missy settled inside the building, Lieutenant Yancy served hot, steaming coffee to his guests, making sure to put an extra amount of canned milk in the cup for Missy.

Moved by Carie's story, Yancy could not have been nicer, until John Revell entered the room with Meri and the sergeant.

"Ma'am," said the Ranger, "the horses are all watered, and High Cloud has taken them out about a mile south to graze. The geldings don't seem to be bothering the mares—guess they're too tired."

Before Carie could respond, Yancy's good manners vanished and his expression hardened as he glared contemptuously at Revell. "Sergeant Rainwater, arrest this man! And call in a guard to detain these women."

The abrupt change in Yancy's behavior so startled Carie that she was momentarily speechless.

The soft, southern drawl of Sergeant Rainwater advised, "Oh, I don' think I'd do that, suh, 'cause this here's Gen'ral Revell's nephew."

Yancy, paling considerably, stared wide-eyed at his sergeant and whispered, "You mean our commanding officer at Fort Bliss is the uncle of this rebel?"

Before the sergeant could reply, John stepped forward, saluted smartly, and said, "Yes, sir! I am General Revell's nephew, sir, and may I introduce myself? Major General John Revell, late of the Army of the Confederate States of America, and presently a duly appointed Texas Ranger licensed by the great state of Texas." Without hesitation, the Ranger continued, fairly shouting, "And what's more, sir, the war is over!"

Missy couldn't have said it better in one breath. Yancy's legs failed him, and he collapsed into his chair. John looked disgusted. Missy put her hand over her mouth to suppress a giggle. Meri's eyes beamed with adoration, and Carie's steely eyes never left Yancy's face.

Carie finally spoke. "Excuse me, Lieutenant Yancy. This has been my fault. I would have been madder'n hell if somebody dumped 200 horses in my front yard and let them drink water I'd hauled in from forty miles away." She paused but not long enough to allow Yancy time to answer. "But, please understand, Lieutenant, my husband and my son served as loyal soldiers for four years in the same uniform you're wearing. Mr. Revell, here, felt his loyalties lay with the South. This tragic situation happened all across our great nation—brother against brother. Thank God, Lieutenant, that the war is over and we are all again under one flag. Am I correct, sir?"

Lieutenant Yancy was able only to murmur, "Yes, ma'am," for the molten gray eyes fairly shot sparks that held him tongue-tied.

Carie never let up, however. "I just need to know one thing, Lieutenant Yancy. We had been discussing your troop helping rescue my husband and son. Can I depend on you?" she demanded.

This demand hit home, and Yancy bounded to his feet, "Oh, yes, ma'am."

Carie's face softened into a brilliant smile. "Name's Carie. Thank you, Lieutenant Yancy. We'll leave about two hours before daybreak tomorrow. Will you be ready?"

Looking stricken, he again croaked, "Yes, ma'am." And then he barked, "Sergeant!"

No further business to be discussed, Carie spun and hurried to the door. Her crew followed, except for

Missy, who looked into the large black eyes of Sergeant Rainwater. "I surely do like your uniform, sir. Mighty lot of stripes on your sleeve, and I've never seen so many medals! My pa was a major; lost his left leg at Gettysburg. Grandpa saved his life. Johnny Reb shot it off. Wasn't this Johnny Reb, though. This one was my pris'ner, but he's a pretty good guy now. Grandpa was a major gen'ral, but he didn't have a lot of stripes like you, neither. They'll be real glad to get to meet you!" Missy drew in a deep breath and smiled brilliantly at the equally delighted black man.

The sergeant, almost overcome with glee, gently clasped the child's hand and led her quickly out the door. "Let's go fix up that sore shoulder, little missy, and you can tell me all about it."

As they departed, the dejected Lieutenant Yancy again collapsed into his chair and, elbows propped on the desk, put his head down into his hands.

6

VVVVVV

The Ranger

THE HEAVENS BLINKED a
starry welcome through the chill darkness as the
McKittrick crew, joined by the buffalo soldiers, scurried
to get chores done, making ready for their early morning departure.

The evening before, Sergeant Rainwater had respectfully asked Carie to allow Missy to go hunting with him,
and the two brought back a large sackful of plump blue
quail. The entire camp enjoyed a sumptuous supper of
fried quail and gravy, along with the usual bacon and
beans. As an added treat, John and the camp cook prepared a pot of stewed apples and biscuits. The festive
evening not only filled empty bellies but was also
enhanced by Missy's tales of her new "hero," Sergeant
Rainwater. She crowed of his skill as he shot each quail
in the head instead of the body, " 'cept maybe just one

of 'em. Sure is easier eatin' when you don't have to pick buckshot out'n your teeth!"

Meri's soft brown eyes danced as she listened to her sister, but throughout the evening, they drifted more and more to the Ranger. Carie herself even relaxed a bit and chuckled when the precocious child proudly announced that "her fren'" was also the "bestest doctor in the whole worl' 'cuz he fixed my shoulder and now it doesn't hurt a'tall!"

Before dawn, with the horses saddled, the troops' mules harnessed, and old Hammer, free of his burdens which were now stowed in a wagon with the other gear, stood patiently waiting as the group wolfed down a huge breakfast. No matter that they had eaten so much the night before, each knew that aside from a dry biscuit, a chew or two of jerky, and a few sips of water from a canteen, that would be all they would have that day until after dark.

Carie had been sharing a seat on a large log with the now congenial Lieutenant Yancy. She was the first to rise from the meal. "High Cloud, take the right side of the road and I'll take the left. Girls, send the mares in behind us. The troops can follow the mares. Ranger, you drop in with the geldings."

Lieutenant Yancy, only too glad to permit the dynamic little lady to take command, barked, "Sergeant, have the men fall in!"

Carie handed her plate to the camp cook, saying, "Enjoyed the meal," and turned to Missy. "I saddled your grandpa's Pelote for you." The little girl's jaw dropped and her eyes lit up as a joyful grin spread over her face.

The sergeant's command, "Stand by to mount!" was followed by the sounds of metal clanging as the soldiers quickly dropped their tin plates into the cook's wooden tub and hurried to their picketed mounts now shuffling in anticipation. No one spoke, except for Missy who, upon finding her voice, started telling everyone within earshot about her flashy grulla, Pelote.

Boots, being one smart dog, assigned himself. He jumped into the wagon, crawled under the wagon seat, curled up and promptly went to sleep.

High Cloud's whistle pierced the air, signaling to move 'em out, followed by the sergeant's "Ho-o-o-o!" The little army advanced.

By noon, the sun had broken through the clouds that lazily drifted to the northeast, promising a shirtsleeves day.

Carie drew up alongside her adopted son and spoke as she removed her brush jacket and tied it behind her saddle, "High Cloud, we've come over halfway. I think it might be a good idea to stop and rest for an hour. I'll go back and see how everybody's doing. Just you keep a sharp eye on the mares—don't let them wander too far from the road." Moving away, she added, "Wouldn't hurt you to rest a little, yourself. I'll see if our Yankee can send a couple of troopers to help." The Indian sat quietly watching as Carie rode slowly back through the pack of horses for about a mile, to where the wagon and troops were.

Lieutenant Yancy held up his hand to halt his troops as Carie approached and he greeted her. "Anything wrong, ma'am?"

"No, I just thought it might be a good idea to stop

and rest for a spell. I'd be obliged if you'd send a few men forward and have one drop off every 100 yards or so to help my son keep an eye on the horses."

Even though Yancy's eyebrows lifted at the words "my son" instead of "the Indian," he had by now learned not to question the little lady and snapped, "Be happy to. Sergeant! Front and center!"

Sergeant Rainwater spurred his horse and drew alongside Yancy. "Rainwater, take four men forward to watch the horses."

"Yes, sir!" barked the sergeant. "First two by two, move out!" Rainwater and his men trotted off to carry out the order.

The girls rode up, and Carie said, "Best you go help High Cloud, too," and, to their departing backs, added, "Just keep 'em quiet and let 'em graze." Tapping Skye's Son into a trot, she passed the wagon and the remaining troops. As she neared John Revell, she waved and called out, "We're takin' a break, Ranger."

He waved back, acknowledging the command.

Carie reined in her animal and wearily dismounted. She loosened the girth on Skye's Son and removed his bridle so he could graze, hanging the tack on the saddle horn. Massaging her own waist and back, she took in a deep breath, sighed, "Ah-h-h," and walked toward the tall grass clumps that edged the road.

She literally crumpled to the ground to rest—and to think.

Within minutes the Ranger rode up, looked down at her and politely asked, "Mind if I join you?" Tired eyes met his, and with a slight smile, Carie said, "Glad to have your company."

Revell, mounted on Willie's round-backed Bubbles, descended, along with his saddle, which slipped down the horse's side as he dismounted. "Little feller," Revell said to the animal, "for a horse that has as easy a ride as I've ever been on, I can't understand why you have such a round back and no withers at all." This statement brought a wide grin to Carie's face as she looked lovingly at the dun, thinking of her grandson.

As the two sat in companionable silence, so lost in reverie was Carie that she was startled when John softly said, "Tell me about Will McKittrick, Miz Carie; he's got to be some kind of man, because you and your family all quote him at least ten times a day."

Carie's face eased into a soft smile and her eyes regained their sparkle. Her voice, when it came forth, was soft and mellow. "You ask what my husband is like, John—well, after forty-some years you'd think I know everything there is to know about the man." Hesitantly, as though wondering where to start, she chuckled, "Sometimes I know what he's going to do even before he knows; then, at other times, when his Irish temper flares up over what seems almost trivial to me, I am surprised." Raising her head to look at John she said, "It doesn't frighten me, understand, as someone else's anger might. Although Will..." she looked upward and smiled as though she could see her husband before her. "Will says I'm not afraid of anything. Not even the devil himself."

With this, she dropped her chin almost to her chest and muttered, "But I am, though, and right now I am afraid." She raised her eyes again to meet the Ranger's, wordlessly pleading to be understood.

He was nodding. "I know, Miz Carie, but you sure don't show it."

Recovering her composure, Carie continued, "Then there are times when he goes to the opposite extreme and doesn't get mad at all over things I thought he would have." Again her spirits rose and she chuckled, "There is one thing about Will, he does become almost unhinged over protecting his family—and he's a fanatic about working harder and longer hours, just so he can provide us with the very best this country has to offer." Laughing aloud, her face crinkled with deep lines. "I guess that's just from being Irish—if my Will is any indicator of the typical Irishman, then they are deeply passionate and emotional beyond belief. They live hard, work hard, do nothing half-way." Shaking a finger to emphasize her point she said, "To Will, life is the black and white of a checkerboard—there is no gray. That's why, when he told me he was going to follow Billy Frank to El Paso and join the Union army, I *knew* that it wasn't because he didn't love us—nor did he fear for our safety if he went. I *knew* he loved us more than life itself."

Pulling her floppy sombrero down to shade her eyes, Carie continued, "At first, it did come as a surprise to me, until, Ranger, it dawned on me that he was leaving for two wonderful reasons—one"—the stubby little finger pointed forward—"to keep our nation whole, and again protecting it for *us*—protecting the land from being pulled apart by blue, gray, or renegades like the ones that challenge us here and now."

Carie stopped, picked up her canteen to take a long drink, then handed it to John before continuing. "The other reason is that extreme I was just talking about. By using his powerful body, intelligence"—and again her infectious laugh rose from her throat—"*and* his good looks, he believed he could outfight, outwit, or charm *anyone* and was certain he could bring back our beloved son to us."

The Ranger was, by this time, smiling broadly into the lady's face, and he laughed with her as she continued, "And that big galoot *did* bring him home! Well, John, have I answered your question?"

"Yes, ma'am, you sure have."

Carie eased back on her elbows and stretched out her legs. "Oh, but lest you get the idea Will's the perfect man, John, there was only one so good, only one Perfect Man. My Will can be the most stubborn, cantankerous son-of-a-gun that ever walked! Why, I've seen him use not only me, but use Billy Frank, Lea, the kids, and, yes, even the pride of his life, his beloved Thoroughbreds, to a point where we were near to exhaustion. And, if you can imagine, seeming not to care! And *never* saying he was sorry. 'Sorry' is not in his vocabulary."

Seeing the wide grin spreading across the face of her companion, Carie added, "He's hard, rough, tough, but also the funniest man, and the greatest storyteller I ever had the pleasure to be around."

"And you love him," replied the Ranger.

"And I love him. Oh, yes, John, from the first day I laid eyes on him to this very day." Carie grew pensive. "And for many days and years to come. He's a part of me. The way he puts it, we fit. We are one."

With this exchange, the burdens of the past few days seemed to slip away, and her eyes lit up with an impish twinkle. "John, you didn't really sit down here with me to talk about Will McKittrick, did you? I'm thinking that you just might want to talk about Meredith. I've noticed the way you two look at each other. Well?"

This time it was John who was caught off guard, and before he could reply, Carie laughed. "Now before you swaller your tongue, I'm going to say 'yes.'"

A faint flush spread above the stubby growth of beard on the Ranger's cheeks, and he lowered his head as if to avoid Carie's penetrating look.

Knowing full well she had struck a sensitive spot, Carie's voice was gentle. "As to what I feel about it, here's one more story about my Will. When we first met at Pa's livery stable, he felt what I felt, and whether it had been three years, three days, or three hours after we met, we both knew then and there that I'd go anywhere with him, and under any circumstances."

A small frown crinkled her brow, and her steely gray eyes locked into his as he raised his head. "And this is damned important, John, so don't hang your head and blush, because what I'm talking about is the greatest experience the good Lord gave to a man and a woman!"

The Ranger, spellbound, never spoke and never moved.

"Will McKittrick married me aboard a cargo ship, appropriately named the *Good Hope*. In whatever words you choose, Will first made love to me, took my virginity, or made me a whole woman, not in our tiny, thin-walled cabin but down in the hold of that stinking ship, on the straw-covered floor next to the stall of his first great Thoroughbred, Skye. He wanted privacy for us—for me—to protect me from any possible embarrassment from rude and knowing looks of the crew, who might have poked fun at the newlyweds."

Unable to control the beet-red flush again on his cheeks, John remained mesmerized by the most unusual dialogue of his entire life, including those with his own mother. Carie compassionately continued, "Will McKittrick was protecting me and, to make sure of our honeymoon privacy, took me to the one place on the ship where he knew no one but we two would venture — near his mad, wild Thoroughbred!"

Carie and John convulsed with laughter, and as Carie straightened up, her eyes darkened and her face again became somber. "What Will and I have together is what I want for Meri and you, John," she said simply and reached out to grasp his hand.

In a voice hoarse with emotion, John murmured, "I want that for us, too, ma'am," not the least ashamed of the joyful tears he blinked from his eyes.

"Call me Carie." Again they burst into laughter.

At that exact moment two quick rifle shots rang out in the distance, followed by the thunder of many hoofs, frightened nickering, and the shouting voices of men and the girls.

"What in hell. . . ." muttered Carie, as she and the Ranger jumped up and ran for their horses. Tightening the girth, Carie did not bother to put Skye's bridle on but quickly climbed into the saddle. John, who had not removed Bubbles' headgear, picked up the reins and vaulted into the saddle.

As they flew past Lieutenant Yancy, who had climbed into the wagonbed to mimic Boots in barking orders and to try to get a better look at what was going on,

Carie yelled, "LOO-TEN-ANT! Send someone back to handle the geldings while we go see what's happened!"

The Ranger's heart thudded as he marveled at the wiry little Carie deftly guiding her powerful horse with only her knees, while shouting at the troopers.

"And try to stop the mares, and keep them in check!" As she raced past them, one last admonition could be heard, "And be careful in the tall grass, it's full of prairie dog holes!"

The black faces were a blur as the two thundered past. Yancy waved at their departing backs, opened his mouth to bark the orders, but the buffalo soldiers were already acting on Carie's commands.

Since the horses had turned and were running headlong toward Carie, she slowed Skye's pace as she and John approached so as not to spook the horses further in their near-stampede. The stallion nickered, and Carie's voice joined that of the Ranger, "Whoa-a, girls.... Whoa...."

One by one the mares began to slow and turn, as the calming effect of the human voices reduced their panic. Carie was so intent upon calming the frightened horses that she did not immediately notice John wending his way to her side, trying to tell her something. He had to shout to be heard. "Miz Carie!"

Sensing something further might be wrong, she swung the stallion around, and yelled, "What?"

"I said, I can see the girls' horses but I can't see the girls!"

"No need to borrow trouble," she replied, her expression stern. "They know how to take care of themselves." Fear, however, gripped her heart until, when scanning the terrain, she spotted Meri rise from the tall grass and wave to them.

"Oh, thank God!" sighed Revell, spurring ahead.

As they pulled to a stop near Meri, the freckle-faced Missy came crawling out of the grass, muttering, "Damned stickers! Got'em all over me." She brushed and picked at her clothing, oblivious to the concern on the faces of her grandmother and John.

"Meri, what happened?" John asked anxiously, even before Carie could speak.

Meri closed her eyes briefly, took in some air, sighed and moistened her dusty lips before answering, "High Cloud caught two vaqueros trying to rustle some of the mares. One got away, but he shot the other one and he's down, out there, somewhere in the grass, on foot. High Cloud told us to get off our horses and hide, and he's gone after him."

"Your blood brother's a smart lad," Carie said with conviction. Both girls brightened in assent. The Ranger, no longer able to contain himself, hastily dismounted and grabbed Meri, knocking off her hat as he pulled her into his arms. "I was so scared when I couldn't see you!" Meri, overcome with joy, hugged him back.

Looking on with sheer disgust, Missy rolled her eyes heavenward. "Golly, Gran Carie, don't they just make you sick to your stomach?" Carie, however, smiled at the pair and a warm glow swept over her.

The horses and their keepers dozed in the Indian autumn; minutes stretched into an hour as they quietly awaited High Cloud's return. "He's back," Carie said with relief, "and he's alone," as she spotted High Cloud coming over a small hilltop some distance away. As he entered the tall grass, he darted quickly in and out of sight, ever watchful of the ground below or that visible around him over the grassy heights. He had removed his jacket, and his bronzed skin glistened in the sunlight, muscles visibly rippling in torso and legs with every step. As he neared Carie and the others, only his face betrayed his exhaustion.

"I'm sorry," the young Indian apologized to his mother, "I was unable to find the other bandido." Pausing, he frowned as he pondered aloud, "It was strange, because when I found the body of the first man, I could see he had already taken a shotgun blast to the shoulder. The other fell off his horse into the grass; I tracked him as far as the Diablos." He turned to point westward to the mountain range that paralleled the valley, "but in the rocks I soon lost his trail." Shaking his head, again he said, "I'm sorry, Gran Carie."

"No bother, High Cloud, the snakes'll get him." Carie's gray eyes met the golden brown of his, and handing him her canteen, she said, "Here, rest a little. I'll go get a fresh horse for you."

Carie tried to control the new and overwhelming fear that caused her to shudder. No one in the group noticed the involuntary trembling of her hands as she caught the mane of the patient Alice, nor did they hear her whisper into the gray's ear as she slipped a bridle over the mare's head, "Lea. A shotgun—it could only mean Lea." It took all the strength of character she could muster to keep a straight face as her imagination filled with thoughts of Lea. She led the mare back to High Cloud, making sure to look away as she handed him the reins and said gruffly, "Let's get movin'." Then remembering her manners, she quietly said, "Girls, help the Ranger at the rear." Within minutes, Carie set a fast clip, leading the horses and riders toward Adobe Wells, still fifteen long miles away.

The Diablos far behind, the sun was disappearing behind the steep, jagged Eagle Mountains to the west. By the time the lone adobe house came into view, the valley was covered by lengthening shadows of the mountain peaks. An old rock tank near the pole corral held water that reflected a last faint shimmer of light, but it was the suspiciously silent and empty corral that caught Carie's eye. She sucked in a deep breath and uncharacteristically jerked Skye's Son to a stop. Sensing her fright, the horse stomped and threw back his head, shattering the stillness with a loud nicker. From under the sagging roof of the shed came an answering bray— and out of the adobe came Lea, waving a large dish-towel. Carie swayed in her saddle and slumped over the horn in gratitude that her son's wife was safe.

High Cloud shouted, "Hallo-o-o!" and the girls abandoned their duties, racing toward the adobe and Lea. Catching the scent of precious water, the herd too raced ahead, leaving the lieutenant, wagon, and troops in the dust. A totally wild bunch arrived at the large, man-made rock water tank at Adobe Wells.

It was a happy reunion, Lea captivating not only her family, but the officer and his troops, as she told them how she had "discouraged" the outlaws with her shot-gun. Carie did not disclose that she had felt any anxiety; she joined in with the others in happy celebration. But she brought the festivity to an end when she said, "They've got to be the same ones that High Cloud had a run-in with today. But, no need to worry. Let's just bed down early, so's we can get off before daylight." Carie firmly hugged the lovely Lea, and, with a warm, genuinely loving smile said, "Lea, you'll be with that little son of yours by early afternoon."

All would have been well had it not been for Missy, who found the wrong time to open her mouth, "But I don't want to go to bed! I still haven't told Mama about the accident, and Duke falling down the mountain!" In an instant Lea's expression changed—her reproaching eyes flashed anger at Carie.

"What accident, Carie?" she demanded.

Able only to stammer a weary reply, Carie sighed, "Duke slipped and fell. He's dead. Lea, as you can see, the child is fine."

Uneasy silence followed her out the door as she left the dim light of the kerosene lamp and sought the comforting blackness of the night.

It was much later, as the Ranger arose to take his turn at watch, that he passed the blanket-shrouded figure, gray eyes glazed as they stared into the smoldering embers of the campfire. Shocked to see that she was still awake, John's heart swelled in sympathy, and he quietly whispered, "Everything's going to be fine, Miz Carie; everything's going to be just fine." Neither eyes nor body responded. The Ranger paused, then moved quickly into the darkness.

.W.W.\

At about the same time, in the cave at Little Warrior Creek, the sound of loud snores from the outlaws met

the cold of the cave's floor. Will couldn't decide which
was worse—the days or the nights. The long, drawn-out
days were monotonous, but the nights made him want
to shout in anger at his captors. As if the crude, rough
leather thongs that bound his hands and feet weren't
enough, they confined him in a cramped, uncomfortable
position. In addition, Will exerted a constant effort to
stay awake and vigilant while Billy Frank slept; he kept
his large body snuggled up close to his son to conserve
body heat for them both. Through the night, the only
thing Will had to distract him or to look forward to was
counting the minutes and hours till just before dawn,
when the wily little Oriental would surreptitiously bring
them food, coffee, and the foul-smelling balm for Will's
injured hand.

This night had to be the worst yet, he thought,
because the monotony was getting to their captors as
well. After taking turns watching over the herd, the row-
dies had little to do except souse themselves into a stupor by drinking *pulque* or playing card games, or worse,
amusing themselves with their murderous game of bet-
ting on their skills with knives—their favorite targets
being Will and Billy Frank.

In the bandits' drunken state, it was a sheer miracle
that neither McKittrick had been killed. Thankfully,
aside from the terror and humiliation, the two had suffered only a few nicks on their bodies—saved mainly by
the heavy brush jackets they wore. Each savage slice into
the cloth, however, let in more of the chill air, and
hence, each cold night became more unbearable.

So it was, when the little cook came to minister to
them, Will's teeth were so clenched he could not speak,

and it was Billy Frank who first rose to accept the hot coffee brought by the bobbing little man. "Thanks so much, friend," he said, taking the cup and handing it to his father, "but I sure wish you'd be more careful. If Gomez catches you, you'll be in a hell of a lot of trouble." The mute bowed and bobbed, again favoring them with his grotesque, toothless grin before he scurried back to the campfire.

As the simple man reached to pick up bread freshly baked in the giant Dutch oven, he lost his balance and fell. One knee hit the searing pot, and the other fell into the hot coals. An ear-splitting scream arose from his throat, rousing even the drunkest of the bandidos from stupor. But it was Gomez who first shot up from his pallet, yelling at the cook who was dancing around trying to brush out the flames on his coat, "*Carramba!* You stupid Chink!" He rushed forth and mercilessly raised his quirt, striking the poor man. Gomez would have continued flogging until he had slain him, but for one of the less intoxicated men who rushed to pull down Gomez's arm and urging, "*Jefe*, no! *Jefe*, he's the only cook we got!"

At the back of the cave, Billy Frank lay across the struggling body of his enraged father, in a hushed voice quietly pleading, "No, Papa! No-o-o!"

/\/\.\/\

Feliz looked down at the tear-stained, bruised, and dirty little face of the sleeping Willie. "*Pobrecito!* My little amigo, he suffers much. I will be thankful when his mama and the *patrona* come." As though his voice had

been lifted as a prayer to The One on High and immediately answered, across the canyon and around the hill
came first a black horse, then a bay, then the entire
majestic, thundering herd.

Feliz gently shook the sleeping child, "Wake up!
Wake up, Willie! They are here!"

Willie's bloodshot eyes squinted as the two puffy slits
opened and immediately brimmed with tears. He
groaned and rolled over onto his stomach, hiding his
face with his arm.

"I told you, Feliz, I don't want to see them," the
youngster moaned, "and I don't want them to see me!
I kilt Gran Carie's horse!" Willie sobbed into the rocky
ground.

With a sigh, Feliz removed the bandana from his
neck, stepped out from the shade of the scrubby cedar
and wildly waved the red flag at the approaching riders.

Lea, who had earlier climbed bareback onto the
placid Operator, was the first to spot Feliz. She bolted
forward, leaving the others behind as she crossed the
distance separating her from her son. Carie grinned at
the sight of Lea racing toward Willie and, to no one in
particular, said, "Never thought I'd see Lea ride like a
wild McKittrick; but, then, she *is* a McKittrick." Behind
her High Cloud answered simply, "That she is."

When Lea reached the hillside where her son lay
moaning, her look of joy faded to alarm, and she anxiously turned to Feliz asking, "What has happened to
him?"

Feliz, shaking his head as if to clear away all thoughts
of the near loss of the boy, almost choked on his reply.
"Carrasco's man shot Chance, and when the *caballo*

141

fall—Willie, he knocked out." Attempting to reassure the distraught mother, he added, "But, truly, Señora Lea, he is well—not hurt badly. He is just *muy triste* for the *caballo.*"

Lea said no more, but pulled the child to her breast and cradled him, gently rocking. Carie stayed busy getting horses and people settled on the grass-rich canyon floor. The troopers were already setting up camp, and soon the smells of wood smoke mixed with the aroma of coffee drifted aloft with the soft evening breeze. Meri and Missy had gone to join their mother and Willie. By the time Carie was finally able to leave camp, she was surprised to see Missy come running, hell-for-leather, to meet her.

"Missy, it's not right to run a tired horse when you don't need to," she greeted her crossly, frustrated with the child.

Missy's frazzled little face surprised her grandmother when the child nodded in agreement. "Oh, Gran Carie, I'm sorry, but I was just goin' to get a canteen of water from the wagon for Mama. Willie's been hurt and he's cryin', somethin' terr'ble!"

Shocked, Carie couldn't immediately answer. She finally found her voice. "Run on, child."

Missy spurred her mount on to the wagon.

With barely a touch of Carie's spurs, Skye's Son lunged forward to race to the hilltop. As the big black slid to a stop, Willie was still in his mother's cradling arms, still sobbing, his face hidden from Carie.

As Feliz reached to catch the black's reins even before Carie's foot hit the ground, he was telling her what had happened. Lea looked up at her mother-in-law with bitter condemnation but said nothing.

Carie dropped to her knees and with both hands gently pulled the child's face around to hers. Seeing the puffy eyes, the scrapes and bruises on Willie, shock and dismay punished her. Finding the will to mask her pain, she said firmly, "William Franklin McKittrick the Third, stop your bawling! I'd gladly give up ten like Chance *any* day, just to have you around!"

Lea was so stunned she willingly, almost gratefully, let Carie pull her grandson into her lap. Willie's slight smile came, as it always did, and his black eyes glistened up into Carie's face with relief. "Would you really, Gran Carie?"

As the two gazed happily into each other's eyes, Missy returned with a rousing clatter, not with the canteen, but with a large pail of water, half of which had most likely sloshed out during her wild ride across the canyon. Close at her heels was Sergeant Rainwater, carrying a black medic's bag.

"Willie!" shouted the little girl, so loudly that even the highly trained Skye's Son shied away. "This here's Sergeant Buck Rainwater. He's a real big import'nt sol'-jer, and he's been doctorin' with a surgeon in Virginny, so I know he kin fix you up real good. Rainwater ain't no Injun name, he's called that after a plan-tay-shun at someplace called Ally-bammy. They just call him Buck." Her beatific smile seemed to spread over her entire body as she diverted her attention from Willie to the now abashed sergeant, announcing confidently, "He's gonna fix you up, and then Pa and Grandpa Will are gonna be even more glad to meet him!"

As Missy took in a deep breath, smiles appeared on the women's faces for the first time since they arrived.

The sergeant knelt to tend his small patient, and his deep voice rolled, "You be right as rain when I gets through wit' you, Master Will."

Only then did Willie attempt a wide smile. Missy beamed.

/\/\/\

It was the terror of her dreams that woke Carie before dawn the next morning. All she could remember was that she had been running, running, and no matter how fast she ran she couldn't reach her goal. So real was her nightmare panic that she awoke with a start, sitting upright, her heart pounding. And, as chill as the early morning was, her body was bathed in perspiration. Wearily, she threw back the blanket and reached for her hat. "Lord, I hate this sombrero," she muttered, but she yanked it down onto her head, got to her feet, and walked to the campfire.

She had just poured a cup of coffee when she sensed the presence of someone behind her. Startled, she turned to call out just when Feliz came ambling into the firelight.

"*Patrona*, I am sorry, I did not mean to scare you."

"No matter, Feliz, I'm just a little jumpy. We're so near to Will and Billy Frank. I wish we could just—just ride out right now and get them!"

The old fellow smiled at his mistress, "We go when you say, *Patrona*."

"Tomorrow," was the terse reply.

Feliz poured himself a cup of coffee, but, rather than straightening up, he hunkered down into a squat and stared into the fire. "*Patrona, perdona me,* please be care for you'self." When no answer came, the old man arose.

From behind him he heard, "I will, Feliz. Don't worry, I'll be careful." The two old friends sat in comfortable silence, waiting for daylight.

High Cloud and the Ranger rode up, coming in from their duties as night-hawks. Carie brightened at the sight of her two friends, "Mornin', boys!"

"Mornin', Miz Carie."

As they began to unsaddle their mounts, Carie said, "Would you mind if I ask you to wait a spell to tend your horses? I need to talk with you before the girls get up."

"You bet," replied the Ranger, already ground-tying his horse.

"Oh, and High Cloud," she spoke to her Indian son, "see if you can roust out the lieutenant. We'll need him, too."

Within minutes he returned with the sleepy-eyed Lieutenant Yancy, who was positioning his suspenders over the top of the reddest pair of longjohns Carie had ever seen. She couldn't help but chuckle and didn't dare look at John, who buckled over in a fit of 'coughing.' By the time the two reached her she was smiling pleasantly, "Good morning, Lieutenant Yancy."

"Morning, ma'am," he gruffly replied. "Something wrong that you be needing me?"

"Why, no, lieutenant, I just thought that now might be a good time to put our heads together as to how I figure we can get my husband and my son."

"Well, now, ma'am, the U.S. Army will do that for you," Yancy told her in a patronizing tone.

Carie was so taken aback at this puffed-up young man

that she could not help but grin. Mimicking him, "Well, now, that sure is nice, but the way I figure it, we're *all* going to have to work *together*."

It was the two sets of eyes alongside the lady that stopped Lieutenant Yancy from further offense—two bronzed ones pierced like an arrow and two brown ones sent daggers. Yancy just poured himself a cup of coffee and sat down.

The four men sat quietly; the flicker of fire danced in Carie's eyes, turning them into what appeared to be pure crystal. No one interrupted her, and no one spoke—they just listened intently. At last, she paused and asked, "Well, what do you think?"

They seemed surprised at the simplicity of her plan, but they agreed to it. Even the lieutenant, who said grandly, "Miss Lea and the girls take the mares; High Cloud, the geldings; Mr. Revell, the cattle; my men and I work on the renegades! Couldn't be better!"

"Well, now, I'm mighty glad you approve," Carie replied with a tinge of sarcasm, "but I have one more thing to do. I'd best go tell Lea and see what she thinks."

From behind Carie came the voice of her daughter-in-law, "No need, Carie, I heard it all." Lea walked into the light of the fire. Tears brimmed in her soft brown eyes as she added, "And my thanks for taking care about the children." Hugging Carie, she softly said, "Won't be long now and we'll have our men back."

Carie's eyes also welled with tears, and she quickly turned about, holding her hands out to the fire for warmth, her face set with determination.

"I'd appreciate it if everyone would check the gear,

and all the horses; those that might not be fit to go, take them down to the little spring and hobble them. The rest of 'em —just let them graze." Looking up at High Cloud she said, "Son, we have a little something we need to do. Won't be gone more'n a couple of hours, folks. Come on, Boots." The dog jumped up to follow as his mistress walked briskly away.

Instead of catching the hobbled stallion, Carie walked up to Hammer and slipped the snaffle into his mouth. "I hope you're good and rested, Hammer, because you're going to be mighty important to me this day. The red mule let out an ear-splitting bray in reply. High Cloud chuckled as he saddled Fargo.

"Could you find everything I asked for?" Carie quietly asked the Indian.

"Yes, ma'am," came the soft reply.

"Good. Let's go," she said, and they mounted to ride back up the road from where they'd come the day before.

As they rounded the point of the hill above the small valley, Carie spoke to the young brave at her side. "Do you recall seein' a beehive in the rock bluff of the ravine we passed yesterday, about three miles back?"

A pleasant smile covered the young man's face, "Yes, ma'am, I thought at the time, a little of the sweetness of the great bee would taste mighty good."

"Well, that's where we're going."

High Cloud nodded acknowledgement, but without understanding.

With a curious smirk on her face, Carie continued, "First thing, though, first we've got to find a skunk for Boots."

This time, High Cloud's usual stoic expression crumbled into wonder, and he asked, "A skunk? But why?"

His voice faded as Carie spoke sharply, "Go get 'em, Boots!" and the happy border collie bounded away, sniffing at one rock after another. He spied a large jackrabbit as it darted out from around a small bush, but Carie called him back, "No, Boots!" The dog stopped in his tracks, his ears perked and obedient to Carie's voice. She again ordered, "Go get 'em, Boots!" This curious exercise was repeated a number of times when, a short time later, Boots found his quarry and ran to make his kill. Soon the wretched smell of skunk musk permeated the air, the unbearable stench trapped in the heavy morning fog.

"Phew!" muttered High Cloud.

"Ugh," Carie's face was grim but victorious. "That ought to do it." She called to the foul-smelling Boots as he rubbed his nose and body into the tall grass in an attempt to liberate himself from the stench. Even old Hammer brayed his disapproval, but Carie spurred his side hard. "Shut up, you old fool," she said, and they continued down the draw.

Later, as she and High Cloud stood looking at the beehive, Carie said, "Light the torch I asked you to bring." High Cloud did so, holding it directly under the hive. Black smoke rose around it, and it took Carie just minutes to fill two small pails with honeycomb. Stepping away, she said, "That's good. Now, let's go back down the draw. We'll sit under the overhang of that bluff for a spell; it'll feel good to get out of this cold breeze. There's still a few more things we've got to talk about, anyway."

They scrambled up the bluff and seated themselves near a huge fallen tree, petrified eons ago and now vine-covered. Its leaning trunk jutted out, forever held captive by the rock formations of the bluff.

"High Cloud, get out that salty meat grease I asked you to bring, and let's rub some of it on this old poncho, and rub on some pitch-black from the torch, but save a little for my hair."

The young man's brows lifted in unspoken question, but he complied.

When the task was finished, Carie whistled to Boots, who had been so ashamed of his smell that he had remained some distance away. On hearing Carie's signal, Boots reluctantly crept to her, head bowed and tail tucked between his legs. His odor was so sickening that both Carie and High Cloud had to swallow hard and hold their breath to keep the bile from rising to gag them.

"Come here, boy; good dog," cooed Carie as the poor dog slunk into her arms. She gently rubbed the poncho all over him; soon the poncho was also rank with the smell of skunk, and the dog was as greasy as the poncho. She then slipped the poncho over her head and adjusted it around her small shoulders.

Looking into the eyes of the young brave, she commanded, "High Cloud, swear on the grave of your father, the great chieftain. Swear that you won't move to stop me, no matter what you see next. Swear!"

Pain swept across his gentle brow, and the brave ducked his head with concern, but he gruffly replied, "I swear."

Barely waiting for his oath, Carie was up and flinging

her body—face first—against the dead tree. High Cloud yelled, "No-o-o!" as she staggered back, but her self-inflicted punishment wasn't over. She grabbed the rough trunk and, again and again, rammed her face forward.

High Cloud could not contain the sound that escaped his throat as Carie slumped to her knees and clasped her trembling hands over her face. He rushed to her side, moaning, "Oh, Mother Carie, why have you done this?"

Carie never moved from her kneeling position as she shook her bowed head from side to side. Trickles of blood seeped through her fingers to land in droplets on the flat rock she knelt upon. She shuddered, and in a weak, hoarse voice said, "Build me a fire, and then go down and get Hammer. Bring him up here and tie him to this dad-blasted tree. I'll need my canteen and my bedroll." She raised her head and dropped her hands from her face, her eyes now meeting the horrified stare of High Cloud.

He gasped at the sight of the bruised and lacerated forehead, the swollen nose streaming with blood, both eyes swelling and beginning to blacken. But it was the blood that brought tears to his eyes, blood still trickling down her face onto the filthy, stinking poncho.

As he gently carried her to a warm, dry place near the bluff, she weakly scolded him through clenched teeth, "Now go! Do what I have told you to do!" Carie closed her eyes and tried to go with the pain, but she never moved until High Cloud returned. He scurried to tie Hammer and quickly built a fire.

Though mystified and disapproving of the entire

affair, High Cloud gently touched her shoulder, saying, "Mother Carie, the fire is but six feet away. Let me help you closer to it." Without waiting for an answer, he again picked her up and gently laid her near the cheerful, popping blaze.

"Please tell me, why have you done this, Gran Carie?" he asked quietly, using her pet name.

She opened the puffy slits covering her bloodshot eyes and, by sheer will power, kept them open as she replied with conviction, "It was the only way I could think of to disguise myself, so as to get into Gomez's camp. Now go! You can explain to the others what I have done, but let Lea handle telling it to the children."

She reached out as though to touch her son's face but seeing there the painful horror, she instead rested her hands against her chest, closed her eyes and said again, "Go, my son, go."

High Cloud protested leaving her, but she waved him off and sternly repeated, "Go! I'll be in Rustlers' Cave before midnight. You must be there with the horses an hour before daybreak!"

The worried young man nodded and reluctantly got to his feet. He stood looking down at the little woman, and as he finally started to leave, he could hear her voice trailing after him, "Thank you, dear son. Forgive me for putting you through this, but you are the only one strong enough to have helped me. Oh, and take a pail of that honey back to camp."

High Cloud gagged as he heard those last words, and he ran as if his life depended upon it. He vaulted onto the back of the startled Fargo and spurred him into a blistering run. He raised his bare head to let the cold wind blast against his face as tears streaked back into his hair. Lifting his face to the sky, he screamed, "I swear on my father's grave, I will never again eat the sweet of the great honey bee."

7

VVVVV

Will McKittrick

BILLY FRANK had his hands full all day trying to curb his father's rage, while at the same time marveling at the strength of the older man. The years had not been easy on Will McKittrick, yet when times were especially tough, the massive body and mind joined to outfight, or when need be, to outwit any man half his age. Not a day passed that Billy Frank didn't recall Will's face in the red light of the battle, standing over him, shouting above the deafening roar of cannon, gunfire, and the screams of thousands of men and animals, "Hang on, son! I'll get your horse off you and have you out of there in no time!" And, undaunted by the madness and mayhem around them, he had done just that. His giant body, seemingly with no effort, had rolled the dead mount away from Billy Frank's crushed leg and, even though the son equaled his father in height, the older man easily lifted and carried him from the battle-field. Weeks later, after Billy Frank had endured his worst pain and torment, he tried to imagine just how his father could have accomplished such a feat. But now, his thoughts were interrupted by Will's gruff voice.

"There's got to be a way to get that sawed-off son-of-a-gun."

"Papa," Billy Frank chuckled, "You haven't a snow-ball's chance in hell."

And, as he'd witnessed so many times before, he saw a twinkle replaced the fire in the black eyes, and a smirk crossed the square cheekbones. "Wouldn't mind a little of hell's heat right now!"

The day dragged on for the two men. But their spirits lifted when, as the sun began its descent, the cook, his body bent by the heavy load of firewood he carried, appeared at the mouth of the cave.

"See, Papa," whispered Billy Frank, "I told you he was okay. That quilted kimono coat he wears was bound to have protected him."

"Har—rumph!" was the only audible reply, but the black eyes followed the Chinaman for the next hour as he fixed the evening meal.

It was Billy Frank who observed that the outlaws had little to say as they crammed down their food without conversation. Other than following the orders of *El Jefe*, little or no intellect was required of the wretches. Among them was one, thankfully, who had a little sense, and as the jug of *pulque* was being passed around, he suggested to the hombre at his side, "Get your guitar and let's have a little music."

So, as the haunting strings were strummed, and the Latino voices were joined by the deep ones of the Anglos, the cold cave took on a semblance of sanity. Even Will pulled himself up and leaned against his hard rock pillow to listen.

Billy Frank's heart swelled to almost bursting at the memories of his precious Lea, who, from their courting days, had played and sung for him. Her sweet voice was like that of an angel.

/\\.\\/\\.\\

Carie lay in a tense, cramped knot under the offensive poncho, trying to will her head to stop aching. But the pain, along with the mixed smells of blood, skunk, and grease, proved too much for her stomach; she rolled onto her side and heaved, time and time again. With one final choking gag, the last of her stomach fluids came spewing from her mouth. As the wave of nausea passed, she lay back, not bothering to wipe the newly added foul mess from her chin. She did not dare open her throbbing eyes, but instead lay in stillness until, with the warmth of the fire, exhaustion brought the relief of sleep.

The sun had cast deep shadows into the ravine when Hammer became restive at being tied for so long. He began to stamp his feet and move about, which roused Carie. For a few seconds she didn't know where she was, but as she tried to open her eyes, a sharp pain throbbed through her brain, causing her to suck in a quick gasp of air, holding it until the pain eased.

"Hope I haven't overdone it," she thought, "but I've got to get going."

Moving ever so slowly, she again rolled to her side and tried to open her swollen eyes. Slits of light filtered to her brain and she was able to make out the form of her mule. "So far, so good." But it took another ten minutes to get to her feet, where she stood trembling dizzily. Had it not been for Boots, Carie might not have been able to move. The dog, troubled by the strange behavior of his mistress, had the entire afternoon stayed curled up at her feet, so was near her side when she finally managed to stand. Not being able to see him, she moved her right foot to steady herself and stepped on one of his toes. Boots let out a loud yelp, so startling Carie that she instinctively moved toward the one thing she could see — the blurry outline of Hammer. Momentum carried her forward and she grabbed the red hide for support. Her hands found his neck and she leaned gratefully against the faithful animal. She gulped in deep breaths of the cold air and, as her body began to respond, Carie's hands slowly moved to the mule's head, found the reins and felt her way to the tree where they were tethered. She easily slipped them loose and, still patting the mule's neck, her shaking hands found the stirrup. It took even longer to get her foot into the stirrup. With the help of the saddle leathers, she pulled her battered body onto the saddle.

Strangely, as she settled into the seat, relief flooded over her and she was able to ride easy as Hammer took cautious steps down into the draw. Fortunately, Little

Warrior Creek lay over the hill from the rock bluff, so Carie, though barely able to see, was able to guide Hammer to it. There she turned him easterly up the winding bed of the creek, and toward her destination—Rustlers' Cave.

Carie was no doubt correct in thinking that the extreme measure she had taken to disguise her appearance was, in fact, the only way she might possibly infiltrate Gomez's den. The cave itself was twenty feet above the dry creekbed, accessible only by one lone trail upward from the creekbed to the cave's opening. It could not be reached from either side or from above, because of the huge, ten-foot-thick overhang. From a distance it looked like a huge bowl that had been tipped sideways and stuck into the ground.

The extreme idea was born of her years of experience and training for survival in this harsh country. Carie brought to bear every single scrap of knowledge she had gleaned about the people, the animals, and the land. She was also convinced that only a woman might penetrate the male-guarded fortress. A disguise was needed for two reasons: one, she didn't want to risk being raped or beaten, hence the skunk smell, soot, and grease to discourage close contact with anyone. Her eyes were her most distinctive feature and presented the biggest problem, so she deliberately injured her face to achieve distortion of her fine features. Appearing to be a smelly old hag would intimidate no man and would arouse neither interest nor suspicion. The second reason was contingent upon the first; she needed to get inside in order to forewarn Will and Billy Frank of their imminent rescue and to provide them with weapons. She could not conceal a gun, but she could and did carry and conceal knives; two skinning knives tied to each leg, and, for good measure, another inside her doeskin shirt—for her own use.

The cold, damp darkness was a godsend for her, keeping down the further swelling of her eyes. When she reached the mouth of the long bend leading to the cave, she stopped. Anticipation and adrenalin rushing, she quickly dismounted and tied Hammer to a lone mesquite. Taking a moment to pat Hammer's neck, she whispered, "Go, Boots," and set off, this time following the dog, using the blurry sight of his white hair as a guide up the trail. Boots barked as Carie was intercepted by the lookout nearest the cave. Holding up the pail of honey, she croaked, "I am the bee woman. I have been injured and I need shelter for the night."

The honey made a much greater impression on the man than did her disguise; something sweet was almost non-existent in this part of the country, so he said pleasantly, "Follow me, bee woman." Firelight escaped from the mouth of the cave, dimly lighting their steps, and the sounds of guitar and singing drifted forth as the sentinel led Carie over the rocky steps upward. Before they stepped inside, she was almost shocked to observe that her burly guide was Anglo. He stopped her at a point near the cave's opening and growled, "Give me the bucket of honey and remain here, bee woman. I will go to ask Gomez if he will give you shelter for the night. But," the outlaw added as he received his first whiff of her foul odor, "I doubt that he will, because of the smell you carry and the stink of that miserable animal you call a dog."

As he walked away, Carie strained to squint at the men clustered around the campfire in the center of the cave. Some played cards, but the largest group was gathered around the guitarist, singing in perfect harmony. She had long felt there was nothing more hauntingly beautiful than the songs of the passionate, emotional Mexicans, for they could feel the words as well as the music.

Carie's body tensed as she was able to make out the lookout speaking and gesturing to a gaudily dressed man playing cards. She reached to pull her sombrero lower as the flashy figure rose and turned to look at her; he then walked toward her, strutting like a peacock.

"The gringo tells me you need shelter from the night, bee woman. It is evident from your face that you have been injured, but tell me, why did you come to this place?" Stopping in front of her, he wrinkled his nose and sniffed, then quickly stepped back. "Aye, *carramba!* You smell of the skunk!"

"Oh, magnificent one," screeched Carie, "when I caught my greedy partner in the act of stealing all of the honey we had gathered for many days, he struck me with a log from the fire, knocking me senseless. My faithful dog came to my rescue by licking my poor face. It was not his fault that just before he found me he had tangled with a skunk!" (Missy couldn't have done it better.) Boots added to the play-acting by looking up with sorrowful eyes that drooped from beneath the grease and soot.

"Well, I don't ... " but Carie wouldn't let him finish and, pressing her small advantage, dropped to her knees and screeched even louder, "*Andale!* You are Chango

Gomez, the greatest bandido in all of Mexico! All the people speak of your great courage in fighting the stupid gringo. How could I know, when I came to this place for sanctuary for the night, that I would have the great honor of meeting Chango Gomez! Oh, great one ...." She reached out as if to touch him with her filthy hands.

Gomez recoiled, backing away so fast that he almost fell, saying "Well, hm-m-m, for the honey you were so kind to bring, uh, well, leave your stinking dog outside and also your poncho." He sat back down with the card players and said over his shoulder, "If you go to the back of the cave and sleep among the sacks of feed we keep for our horses, maybe that will keep the smell away from us. But make sure you leave early in the morning."

"Oh, I will, Señor! And thank you, Señor. Gracias," Carie groveled. Elated, she thought to herself, *Yes, you pompous bird, we intend to leave very early*, and she bent to hug Boots. Removing her poncho, she laid it among the rocks just outside the cave and said quietly, "Stay, Boots," and watched as the little collie dropped onto the poncho and laid his head between his paws. His eyes never left Carie as she hunched over and, skirting the bandits, walked toward the back of the cavern where the feed sacks lay.

Her heart pounded and skipped a beat when she saw, not ten feet away, the two men huddled together. It was a shame, however, with her vision impaired she could not see that one set of eyes winked at her and the other stared in wonder. So great was her elation at seeing her husband and son alive that she had to steady herself; fighting the desire to embrace them, she allowed her

160

sore, tired frame to sink down between two feedsacks. Overcome by relief and fatigue, tears of joy rolled down Carie's battered little face.

A short time later, a voice commanded, "*Silencio,* hombres! We must now sleep, for it is getting late. Curly! Go with your miserable brother and relieve those with the cows! José, see to the horses!" The three men rose and hurried outside; the rest moved to lie down around the dying fire. It wasn't long before the three lookouts who had been relieved of their duties joined them. Soon only snores or the shifting and turning of bodies could be heard in the huge cavern.

From the first moment Will realized that the screeching woman had to be Carie, he worked feverishly with his teeth to remove the leather bands from his wrists. As he gnawed through the last salty thread, he untied those binding Billy Frank, and each went to work on the leather securing their ankles. Consequently, when the snores rose to their usual crescendo, this night the sounds didn't annoy Will at all; he just grinned and, giving Billy Frank a pat, said calmly, "I'll be right back."

For such a large man, Will McKittrick, when need be, could be as silent as a panther, and not even Carie realized he was near until he lay over her, using the sacks on either side to keep his full weight from crushing her. One large bandaged hand covered her mouth while the other reached to tenderly brush away her greasy hair from her ear as he whispered, "My Carie, you look like hell. You smell *worse* than hell. But what I really want to know is what in the hell do you mean by coming here alone?"

Carie turned her head slightly, not knowing whether

to laugh or cry. She hissed, "And just how in hell do you think I could have gotten in here any other way! Besides, there's going to be *a whole lot of people* coming here, plus some U.S. Cavalry, in just a couple of hours! Oh, Will," she said as his lips tenderly found hers.

"Tell me all—quickly, Carie," Will whispered as he raised his head.

Her words came as a torrent as she disclosed her plan. "But, go now, Will! It won't be long!"

Reaching under her long, leather riding skirt Carie pulled the knives from their hiding place against her thighs. When she handed them to Will, he said, "Keep one, Carie. You'll know if we have need of it or not. Now rest, love, while you can. Billy Frank and I will take care of everything from now on." Rising, his cat's feet carried him silently back to their son's side.

/\.\\\\/\

In the small canyon to the southwest, Mother Nature had graced the early morning hours with a dense fog that rose and fell over the hills and plains, inhaling and exhaling her breath to a new day. A heavy dew began to form and glisten on the grass and brush as Carie's army began its work. Only one change had been made in her plan. Upon inspecting the horses, High Cloud and John had found that all except those that were shod now had worn and tender feet, the price paid for the long, hard journey. Therefore, the decision had been made to take the entire herd.

Much to the amusement of the McKittricks and the Ranger, Lieutenant Yancy had the night before ordered his troopers to polish the brass—not only on their uniforms but also on the bridles and tack.

All had to admit, however, that the brass shone brightly in the firelight, and next morning, it made for an impressive sight as the troop, being the first to move out, did so smartly, two by two. What they didn't know (which proved to be a blessing) was that this day's event was to be the lieutenant's first battle under fire.

High Cloud loped off to scout ahead, followed by the Ranger and Willie. Then the horses, urged on by the womenfolk and Feliz, their whistles taking on an eerie quality in the dismal fog. At precisely two hours before daybreak, the Ranger, three women, and the boy met High Cloud waiting by Hammer's side. The troops had swung in a wide arc to approach from the north; they were in position above the cave, but they were neither seen nor heard.

High Cloud spoke softly, "The mule is the Gran Carie's signal to us that she made it safely to Gomez's hideout. I pray it is so." To John he said, "Only two men are keeping watch on the cattle." By the time High Cloud's last word was spoken, the Ranger was already up and over the side of the creekbank.

"Okay, Meri, you and Missy go." High Cloud gestured to them to head out. This time, instead of whistling, the girls clucked to the mares, sending them out on the opposite side of the creek, north toward the mesa. Lea spoke softly to Willie, "Let's go, son." They rode on up the trail, and when the mother felt she had found the appropriate spot to hide her son behind a pile of large rocks, she helped him down and handed him her shotgun. "Willie, you must be quiet, and don't move.

Stay alert and keep watch—if any evil men come your way, point the gun at the sky and shoot. We will hear it, and one of us will come. Do you understand?" Lea gave her child a big hug as Willie nodded and flashed a big smile, then scampered up into the rocks to hide.

When Lea returned to High Cloud's side, all was quiet; Feliz, the girls, and the mares were no longer seen nor heard. The geldings stood together, seemingly asleep. Only Skye's Son, held by High Cloud, seemed nervous as he threw his proud head and ears toward the direction the mares had gone.

"Easy, boy, easy," crooned the Indian, "we won't have to wait much longer." As he handed the stallion's lead rope to Lea, he said, "Take him, I will make ready." The young man dismounted, removed the saddle and blanket from Stretch's back and unlashed the rolled pack from back of the saddle. He unrolled it and withdrew a lethal tomahawk, a pair of moccasins, and a small doe-skin pouch. Only then did his eyes meet Lea's. "Willie okay?" The gentle woman's eyes misted as she gave a quick nod of assent. Satisfied, High Cloud sat down upon a rock and removed his boots and spurs, replacing them with the intricately beaded moccasins. Then opening the pouch, he stuck two fingers inside, withdrawing them to paint two white streaks on each high cheek-bone. Jumping up, he moved to Stretch's side and, by dipping his fingers into the pouch time and time again, painted the horse's long shoulders with similar white stripes.

/\\./\\\\/\\

It hadn't taken John Revell long to spot the cattle; their dark bodies stood out in contrast to the ghostly white mist. Circling wide, so as not to spook them, he soon located the two nighthawks.

"What luck," he muttered, "they're both riding the same horse," which, in West Texas lingo, meant that although each was mounted, they had been caught jawing together in the same spot instead of taking care of business in separate positions.

John pulled Fargo to a stop, quietly dismounted and, bending over, crept toward the two. At approximately ten feet, he straightened upright and ordered, "Don't move or you're dead men."

Of course, the men moved. Curly flailed back in fright, kicking his brother's shoulder, nearly knocking him off his horse. When Curly's blue-and-gray-panted leg flew upward, what John did next was nearly disastrous—he lowered his pistol. "What are you fellers doing with a no-good like Gomez?"

Curly, somewhat recovered and thinking he might have an advantage, raised his rifle—a terrible mistake. A Texas Ranger doesn't back down—he goes forward. With speed like that of a striking diamond-back, John raised his forty-five and blew the rifle to smithereens.

All hell broke loose. It didn't take much to spook the cattle; they were up on their feet and running before John reached the rebels' sides. "Get off your horses and take off your boots," John said, "and put that rifle down easy." He could have saved his breath on that, for the addled man had already dropped the weapon, and both men hastily removed their boots. John jammed the boots under his arm, picked up the rifle and whistled for

Fargo. The horse trotted up and John easily swung up into the saddle. At the top of his lungs, John yelled, "WHOO-HAH!" and the brothers' horses whirled, racing after the cattle. The two gringos ran in the opposite direction as fast as their bare feet could take them.

/\/\/\

When the sound of a gunshot reached High Cloud's ears, followed by John's yelp, he swung onto Stretch's bare back and let out a blood-curdling whoop. Stretch needed no urging and took off, followed by the geldings, which responded to the not-too-gentle persuasion of Lea firing off two rounds of the Indian's rifle.

/\/\/\

The soldiers lay prone on their bellies, strategically placed across the top of the overhang of the cave. They cocked their rifles.

/\/\/\

Now far out onto the flat of the mesa, Meri and Missy herded the mares, their whistles keeping the animals in a tight circle.

/\/\/\

Willie's big eyes widened and he let out a wild yelp as High Cloud and the horses flew past him. The din of their iron-shod hoofs against the rocky creekbed echoed

166

and amplified it to sound like hundreds. As High Cloud reached the sharp bend at Rustlers' Cave, all that the frantic lookout could see was a wild Indian riding a wild horse.

"*Indios!*" he shouted, "*Indios!*" as he headed for the cave.

"Yip! Yip! Yah-h-h!" High Cloud's tomahawk caught the man in mid-back, before he could even reach the steps. Stretch never missed a step in his stride; man and horse thundered past the body and around the bend. Boots took off like a shot to follow them.

Inside the cave it was bedlam. The bandidos yelled, echoing the warning of the now-dead lookout, "*Indios! Indios!*" Nothing struck so much fear in the hearts of men—white, black, brown or yellow—as the fierce Apache who inhabited this part of West Texas. The men had every right to be afraid.

So, it was no surprise to the three figures huddled in the deepest part of the cave to see the renegades run into and fall onto one another. One unfortunate, with bare feet, was pushed off balance and stepped into the fire, yelling, "E-ee-e-Ow-w-w-w!" Long nights spent drinking the *pulque* had so addled the bandidos' brains that many just stood groggily shaking and looking stupidly at Gomez to tell them what to do. Seeing one of them just pull the blanket over his head so enraged the *jefe* that he kicked the huddled bundle. This action seemed to clear his own mind and, thinking of Apaches, he promptly decided it would be best not to stay in the cave only to be smoked out and tortured. He shouted, "Run! Run for your horses!" His night-stained regalia nearly burst its buttons as he yelled at the first men to recover and make a dash for the mouth of the cave. "*Y vamos por las vacas!*" Barely catching hold of one of his fleeing men he told him, "Pietro, stay here and guard the prisoners! You are to kill them if they even move!" Then, with his pistol at the ready, Gomez rushed out of the cave with his remaining men—just at the instant Lieutenant Yancy hollered, "Fire!" The troopers began their barrage from overhead.

As he emerged from the cave, the sight that greeted Gomez was a pitiful bunch of howling, wounded and dying compadres. What happened next was almost too much for the once-mighty *jefe*. Just as two of his *gentes* reached the rope-tied remuda, the McKittrick geldings rounded the curve and thundered down on men and horses alike, scattering the few men left standing. The stampeding geldings broke loose the restraints of the bandits' horses and those trotted after the geldings. Pelote came last, the empty stirrups of Willie's little saddle swinging.

The guns from above were silenced to avoid hitting the McKittrick horses, giving Gomez the edge he needed. Seeing the riderless Pelote, the bandit chieftain grabbed at the grulla's mane, slowing Pelote just enough to swing himself up and into the saddle. Gomez pulled on the reins so cruelly that the horse's sensitive mouth opened in pain; Pelote reared and spun around in the opposite direction. As he headed back west at a run, only two of his mounted men followed Gomez down the dry creekbed—toward Willie.

The lieutenant, flushed and elated, arose from his safe place of cover behind his men and withdrew his saber, raised it above his head and screamed out, "Char-r-rge!"

This proved instantly to be a near-fatal mistake, for at just that moment the first of the renegades topped the shoulder of the creekbed. Had it not been for Sergeant Rainwater, the shot would have hit Yancy dead center, but Rainwater had already lunged for Yancy's knees, and as the gun came up, the shot only grazed his ribs as it went through the fleshy part of his right side. His hat flying, the officer went down, bleeding profusely. Rainwater took over, "Go get 'em, you bunch of swamp rats!" And the proud buffalo soldiers did just that.

Inside the cave, the flickering firelight bathed the walls with an eerie orange glow, as the leering Pietro pointed his rifle at Will and Billy Frank. They could hear the din of battle outside the cave, and Pietro's expression changed from leer to fear. He pulled the lever back on his rifle, saying, "I am sorry, gringos, but I do not think it wise to wait longer to kill you!" As his finger started to squeeze the trigger, Carie chose that moment to rise from her hideaway. In this instant of distraction, two silver blades sailed through the crimson glow, slashing the bandit's throat. As his body crumpled and fell, a huge meat cleaver dropped harmlessly to the floor at his side. Will rushed to Carie's arms; Billy Frank just stared in wonder at the grinning Chinaman, the owner of the meat cleaver.

"Oh, Will!" moaned Carie as he reached her. Neither could speak. Between emotion and tears, they could only gaze into each other's eyes. When Billy Frank recovered his composure, he saluted the Chinaman and hobbled to his parents. Carie pulled Will with her as she flung her arms around her son. The three simply stood and hugged each other, and time stood still.

Their ecstatic moment was short-lived, however, for the bawling of the cattle and their deafening hoofbeats drowned out every other living sound. Will tried to say something to Carie, but the noise was so loud that when she couldn't understand, he just picked her up as if she were a feather and carried her to the fireside. The cook was immediately at her side as Will laid her on a blanket near a pot of bubbling water. Gesturing to the pot, the Chinaman bobbed his head and scurried to his cache of supplies, bringing back clean cloths and, even more surprising, a bar of soap. As Billy Frank looked on with concern, Will dipped the cloth into the water, squeezed it, and began tenderly to bathe the blood and grime from Carie's face.

The roar from outside began to fade, but they heard a new sound—the clatter and crashing of hoofbeats approaching inside the cave. Billy Frank instantly moved, and with speed rarely seen in a man with a wooden leg, grabbed the dead bandit's rifle and turned to meet an attacker. But in came the massive Fargo, eyes rolling, and mouth wide open, lunging to a stop just inches from the crouched figures of Will and Carie.

"By Gawd! Carie, who's that?" shouted Will.

"And on *my* horse!" shouted Billy Frank.

"Why, that's the Ranger," Carie said demurely, beaming at John Revell.

It was Revell's turn to look startled. He stepped down from Fargo, and, grinning sheepishly, removed his hat. "Sure am relieved to see you, ma'am."

As Billy Frank lowered the rifle, Will roared with laughter, "Well, I'll be damned!"

The troopers who had been assigned by Sergeant Rainwater to "Git the Loo-tenant to safety" chose that moment to make their entrance. Lieutenant Yancy stood, a not-too-proud sight, pale as a ghost, with the blood from his wound running down his side, leg, and onto the cave floor. Seeing the large, sharp chin of the huge man by the fire, Yancy instantly knew it was Will McKittrick and, drawing on what remaining strength he had, saluted smartly. "Evenin', General," he said and fainted dead away into the arms of his men.

This was just too much for the Irishman, and his laughter rose as joyful tears streamed down his cheeks. Carie managed a giggle, the Oriental cook made squealing noises, and John Revell and Billy Frank shook hands.

The joyful moment was cut short by the distant blast of a shotgun, echoing down Little Warrior Creek. Carie jumped upward from Will's arms, her swollen eyes meeting Revell's.

"Willie!" they exclaimed in unison.

"Willie? Mama, what do you mean, Willie?" Billy Frank asked anxiously.

"He was supposed to fire the shotgun as a signal if any of Gomez's men came his way," she answered.

Revell was already turning Fargo and preparing to mount, when Billy Frank stopped him, "I'll go, Ranger. He's my son." John looked on as the tall, thin man, with great dignity, hobbled up and said quietly, "Wouldn't mind a leg up, though." The Ranger hesitated, then reached for the bended knee and hoisted. Billy Frank slipped easily into the saddle, turned Fargo, wended his way out of the darkened cave and clattered into the light of day.

Carie eased back onto the blanket and closed her eyes.

Will said gently, "Sleep, my Gran Carie." Then he turned to the Ranger. "My thanks to you, sir, for the care you have shown my family," and, in a voice as big as his body, he boomed out, "and to you fine gentlemen," addressing the buffalo soldiers.

The weakened Lieutenant Yancy never opened an eye. The troopers had applied some of the cook's foul-smelling potion to his wound and tightly bound it. Yancy slept the sleep of the dead, and, as the first snore escaped his mouth, Will's body began to shake. As he raised his head, the lines around his eyes and mouth crinkled in mirth. His black eyes darted to meet those of the startled troopers, then to the grinning cook. No longer able to contain his joy, Will roared in laughter.

The Ranger slowly slid down, curled his legs beneath him, and gazed at Will McKittrick.

.Λ.Λ.Λ

Billy Frank reached the creekbed as High Cloud came racing 'round the bend. Instead of a greeting, they yelled, "Willie!" and raced on, together.

Minutes before, Sergeant Rainwater had regained his tethered mount not a hundred yards from where his men had been stationed atop the cave, and he whipped at the huge cavalry horse as the beast lunged westward at a dead run.

High Cloud and Billy Frank were unprepared for the sight that greeted their eyes.

There was Willie, and he was not alone. There were Lea, Meri, and Missy with Skye's Son, all standing over the battered body of Chango Gomez.

Billy Frank reined Fargo to a stop and leaned over and fell into the arms of his wife. Dancing up and down, Missy started her spiel, "Papa, oh, Papa, you never seed anythin' like it! Skye's Son, when he seed that sorry Gomez on Grandpa Will's horse, it made him so mad that he just up and yanked that ol' son-a-gun plum out's the saddle with his teeth, and pawed him right into th' groun'." She was not only pointing her small finger but also waving her arms in glee. "And, Papa, see over there! Them other two cowerin' by their horses? Well, they just plain give up without a fight! And, oh, Papa, just wait 'til you meet Sergeant Rainwater! He's a wunnerful man! You ain't never seed so many stripes in yore whol' life!" She drew in a breath and continued, "... and, oh, Papa. ..." The happy family dissolved into laughter.

Sergeant Rainwater, his gold front tooth gleaming in the bright rays of the sun, stood above them on the bank, his rifle still smoking from its well-placed shot into the temple of the bandit, Gomez.

As for Carrasco de Monseis, well, the Ranger took care of him.

/.\.\\\.\

So my Daddy Stocks told me!

And, dear reader, I can still see my grandfather, Joe Stocks, rising from my bedside as the first rays of the morning sun filtered through the window glass of that old shack on the ranch at Kent. He'd bend to turn down the wick of the kerosene lamp and gently blow out the flame.

My mother, taking his place at my side, whispered, "Honey, let's try a few sips of water." As I gratefully sipped the sweet mountain spring water, the doeskin-clad feet of Daddy Stocks silently moved to the door. I quickly handed the glass back to Mother and anxiously asked, "But how did he do it, Daddy Stocks?"

However old he was, his back never stooped, and as he straightened, *tall*, he raised his head, smiled knowingly and opened the door. "That's a story for another time, sweetie. 'Must go now and see to the horses."

As I lay back onto the pillows, I could hear the ringing nicker of our old stud greeting his master.

The Author

A daughter of the Drake and Stocks ranching families of San Angelo and the Davis Mountains, Joan Stocks Nobles says she was raised more like a boy than a girl, with a brother and cowboys for her companions. A single mother of three grown children, she has owned and managed hotels and restaurants in Fort Davis and San Angelo. In 1963 she founded High Sky Girls Ranch (now High Sky Children's Ranch). Active in civic affairs wherever she lived, she was named "Mother of the Year" in 1963 by the Fraternal Order of Eagles in Midland; in 1985, the Midland Optimist Club presented her with its "Community Service Award." Wherever she has been, Joan Stocks Nobles has proudly carried her Texas heritage and her love the Davis Mountains and of Thoroughbred horses with her.

The photo was taken by Ann Thoreson.